A Body
Surrounded
by Water

A Body Surrounded by Water

An Inspector Charlie Salter Mystery

by
Eric Wright

Charles Scribner's Sons
New York

Charles Scribner's Sons
Macmillan Publishing Company
866 Third Avenue, New York, NY 10022
Collier Macmillan Canada, Inc.

Wright, Eric.
A body surrounded by water.

I. Title.
PR9199.3.W66B63   1987   813′.54   87-20675

ISBN 0-684-18873-2

10   9   8   7   6   5   4   3   2   1

Printed in the United States of America

For Michael Nader

A Body
Surrounded
by Water

The Micmac Indians called the Island *Abegweit* which means 'Land . . . cradled on the waves'. A hundred miles long and thirty miles wide in the centre, it lies like a scimitar in the Gulf of St Lawrence, near the shores of Nova Scotia and New Brunswick.

When Jacques Cartier saw it in 1534 he called it 'the fairest land 'tis possible to see'. The British won the island from France in 1758 and in 1769 made it a colony. During the American War of Independence, raiders from Marblehead in Massachusetts plundered the capital, Charlottetown, and made off with the colony's Great Silver Seal.

In 1864 the Fathers of Confederation met in Charlotte-town to discuss a united Canada, and in 1873 the Island joined Confederation as its smallest province.

All this is true. In what follows, everything else—the characters and the events—is fictitious and any resemblance to real events and real people is entirely coincidental.

CHAPTER 1

'Even on Prince Edward Island there must be somewhere you can buy free range eggs and chickens.'

They were talking food, had been talking food for an hour over the remains of a lobster stew, followed by Dutch-apple ice-cream and butter tarts. The dinner had been good enough so that they were still sitting around the table at midnight, drinking the bottle of Calvados the guest had brought while they briefed her on how and where to buy groceries on the Island. Through the windows of the cottage, open wide to let the warm night in, came the sound of small waves breaking along the shore; farther off, car doors slammed and Island voices roared their goodnights as the town's drinking lounge shut up its doors.

Charlie Salter and his wife, Annie, were on holiday, guests, once more, of Annie's family. This time, though, instead of occupying the family's guest cottage in Charlotte-town, they were using a house owned by the Montagus in Marlow, a fishing/tourist village forty kilometres away on the north shore, far enough away that Salter did not feel so swallowed up by his in-laws as he had in previous years. They had their two sons with them although the youngest, Seth, spent all his time with his grandparents so as to have daily access to the sailing club his grandfather belonged to. They had, as well, Sheila Tupper, a college friend of Annie's, who was spending her vacation with them, being out of work and between lovers at the same time. Sheila worked in public relations—she had been at various times on the staffs of several publishers, an art gallery, and a television production company that packaged shows for the networks. Tall, pale, her black hair styled in a 1920s style bell, she

was a vivid addition to the Salter vacation household, and
she put Salter's teeth on edge.

On this night they were entertaining Eleanor Vail, a
Toronto writer who was working on a play and had come
to the Island to finish it because she had been offered a
cottage for the summer.

The Salters had never met Eleanor before. The owner of
her cottage, knowing the Salters were staying nearby, had
written to Annie and they had done their duty and invited
Eleanor to dinner. Salter had offered to absent himself for
the meal, fearing to spend an evening in the company of
someone making mental notes for future local colour, but
Annie had been firm, and in the event Eleanor had proved
to be a very pleasant surprise, to Salter at least. She was a
round, soft woman in her early forties, with a delicate fuzz
on her cheeks and upper lip that made her look edible. Her
two or three tiny chins gave her a good-humoured air, and
Salter was not put off by the bright blue tent dress she wore,
recognizing it as the solution of a slightly plump woman to
the problems of fit and style of more conventional clothes.
And besides, such dresses, like bathrobes, create the agree-
able impression that the wearer is naked underneath. Salter
liked her immediately because she treated him as an equal,
ignoring his sex and occupation (that of a police inspector
in the Toronto force), assuming that he was capable of an
intelligent understanding of the conversation of women.

For some time, though, he had been silent as Annie tried
to supply the information Eleanor requested. Where, for
example, was that Toronto staple, pesto sauce, to be had?
And fresh basil? And ricotta cheese? From pasta they moved
to that other staple, mill-ground wholewheat with no addi-
tives. Where could that be found?

'The farmers' market in Charlottetown,' Salter said,
authoritatively. 'It's only open on Saturdays, though. Buy
enough loaves to last a week and freeze them. There's
nowhere else.'

'But half the Island farmhouses advertise homemade bread,' Eleanor protested.

'It's white,' Salter said. 'Better than the packaged stuff, of course, but it's not real bread.'

'Charlie discovered real bread about ten years ago,' Annie said. 'It's baked in Greenbank, Ontario, and brought into the St Lawrence market once a week. Charlie has an understanding with the baker that when he takes his holidays he warns us so that we can lay in a supply to last. I was thinking of having some flown in from Toronto to keep him happy, but he's found this source in Charlottetown that will do.'

Eleanor laughed. 'Maybe I'll make my own. Would you like some if I do?'

'I'll help you bake it,' Salter said.

He picked up the Calvados and gave himself a refill. He considered suggesting that they move on to the porch, but he divined that the good time they were having might have something to do with sitting around the table where they had eaten dinner and decided not to risk breaking it up.

The cottage had been built by a fisherman seventy years before, a small wooden house near the harbour painted blue and grey, designed to look after a working family. In the front, three painted steps led up to the screened porch furnished with rope mats and enough wicker chairs to allow the adults to sit out on Sunday afternoons. The front door opened on to a passageway which gave access to the sitting-room, or parlour, to the stairs up to the second-floor bedrooms, and to the dining-room and kitchen which ran across the back of the house and had its own access to the yard, a door the original owners had used much more than the front door.

Salter's father-in-law had bought the house complete with contents when the widow died, and the dining table was the old family table which might have seated ten for Sunday dinner. Salter and Annie sat at each end, Angus, their sixteen-year-old son, and Sheila were on one side, and

Eleanor sat alone in the centre of the other side. The focus of the conversation had moved around during the early stages of the meal, but by the time dessert arrived Eleanor had it to herself as the group explained the Island to her.

Now Eleanor was asking about free range chickens and eggs.

'You want the lava man,' Annie said. 'I'll tell him to call on you.'

'The lava man,' Eleanor repeated solemnly, as she was supposed to.

'His real name is Tom Gush,' Annie said, 'And that's what we'd better start calling him before he overhears us calling him the lava man. That's Angus's name. You'll see why when he calls.'

Eleanor switched her attention to Angus and waited for the explanation he was agitating to give. From the time of her arrival that evening he had ignored everyone in favour of her as if bewitched. Whatever trick of communication she had employed, perhaps simply treating him seriously, he was now hers, and he wanted to perform for her.

'He lives in a mysterious volcano,' he intoned, in a hushed, doom-laden voice. 'Every day the lava man roams the Island, terrifying the inhabitants with chickens and eggs. Each night he goes back to his volcano to merge with the primitive rock. What is the secret of this strange creature? Is there a mate somewhere in the smoking centre of the volcano where he lives? What ghastly . . . ?'

'Knock it off, Angus,' Salter said. To Eleanor, he said, 'He comes by on Wednesdays. We'll tell him to call on you.'

'I can't wait,' Eleanor said. 'I need someone to do a bit of carpentry work, too. Do you know anyone like that?'

'Diamond Jim,' Annie said. 'He'll look after you.'

'Diamond Jim,' Eleanor said. 'Tell me, does everyone on the Island have a title?'

'Just those two. His name is Jim Brady, hence the nickname. He's a carpenter, and he buys furniture at farm auctions and refinishes it. He can fix anything, and he seems to know everyone. He was the one who told us about Mr Gush, the chicken man.'

'He learned his magical skills from the tree wizard who lives in the forest,' Angus said, grabbing the stage again. 'He is the only one who knows the secret of the lava man. As long as he keeps the lava man's secret, he is safe, but if he ever reveals the ghastly story of the Bride of Lava Man, then the lava man will touch him and destroy him. He's made of wood, and lava man is made of liquid rock heated to ten million degrees Centigrade, so one touch will destroy the wood man.' All this was delivered in a 'who-knows-what-evil-lurks' voice. Angus had recently decided he wanted to be an actor, and he assumed the role of any character his lines suggested. The voice of the story-teller was one of his favourite imitations.

'So how does it come out, Angus?' Sheila asked. 'You can't leave us in suspense, can he, Annie?'

This appeal was designed, Salter guessed, to make Angus aware of someone other than Eleanor, Sheila's claim to her share in the conversation. 'More Calvados?' he asked her. 'Coffee, Sheila?' Annie chimed in.

But they were wasted efforts. Angus was not to be deflected. 'Listen next week,' he intoned when he had Eleanor's attention again, and gave an imitation of dramatic serial-ending music.

When Eleanor spoke again, the table refocused on her. 'In the meantime, how do I get hold of Diamond Jim Brady?' she asked Salter.

'I'll call in tomorrow and ask him to come round to see you,' Salter offered. 'You should have him fix some locks on your doors, too.'

'Here?' Eleanor asked. 'This is Acadia, isn't it? There's no crime here, surely?'

Angus had had time to get wound up again. 'Deep in the

heart of this lovely rural setting a terrible gang of thieves lurked,' he began. But Annie cut him off.

'That's *Ar*cadia you're thinking of,' she said, pleased to correct a writer. 'And there *have* been a lot of robberies. Isn't that right, Charlie?'

'Someone has been breaking and entering the houses along the North Shore.' Salter said. 'There was a spate of it last summer, and now it's started up again.'

'What do they take?' Eleanor asked. 'I've got nothing worth stealing except my typewriter.'

'Nothing special. Money mostly. Whatever they find lying around. Jewellery, of course, and anything that looks valuable and portable. They don't trash the place. And they don't seem to be dangerous—a couple of times they were disturbed and just took off. Mostly, though, they seem to know when someone's not at home. In other words it looks like one of the locals, or a gang of them, who watch for empty houses.'

'I'll hide my typewriter under the bed,' Eleanor said. 'But I'd better get a couple of locks on the doors. All I've got at the moment is a bolt on the front door and the kind of lock on the kitchen door that you open with one of those iron jailer's keys. Now, fish,' she said. 'Where do I buy fish?' She was ticking off a mental list. 'I had fish and chips in a café near Cavendish yesterday. You know what I got? Frozen squares of halibut, shipped in from Toronto. When I looked out the window I could see the boats in the harbour unloading gorgeous fresh cod and there I was, eating neat squares of halibut, packaged in Toronto. It was unreal.'

'Joe 'n' Eddie,' Angus said. 'Right, Dad?'

Eleanor turned her full, womanly attention back to Angus. 'Who are Joe 'n' Eddie, Angus? Do they live at the bottom of the sea?'

'Oh, I haven't heard about these two, have I, Angus?' Sheila asked, turning sideways to face him and nearly getting her shoulder between him and Eleanor.

'They are the Siamese fishermen of Marlow,' Angus began in a lilting, breathless, 'stories-for-children' voice. 'Their mother was a mermaid who was caught in the nets of a young fisherman who lived by himself in a remote village in Newfoundland. He instantly fell in love with her and took her home and kept her in a secret pond at the end of his garden. One day, Joe 'n' Eddie were born, Siamese twins. They lived in the pond with her until one day . . .'

'Where were they joined?' Sheila asked.

'Not where—"how",' he said in a crisp editorial aside. He resumed his story-teller's voice. 'By an invisible bond that no one could see, but if you tried to separate them they both started to die. They looked like men—boys, sorry— but because of their strange parentage they had to stay wet all the time. They could only leave their pond for a few minutes before they began to shrivel up and die. As they grew up and got bigger and bigger, the pond got too small for them and the fisherman knew that one day they would have to leave him. So when they were big enough to look after themselves he wrapped them up in a wet sail—the mermaid, too, because they were her sons and all she had in the world and they wouldn't leave her—and sailed out to sea and put them back in the water. Then he died of a broken heart and the village people never saw him or the boat again. But one day a strange fishing-boat turned up in Marlow Harbour with two men on it. Joe 'n' Eddie.'

'They will sell me some fish, will they? One day?' Eleanor asked.

'Oh yes,' Angus resumed briskly. 'But you have to go down to the harbour, because they cannot leave the sea or they will die.'

'They don't deliver,' Salter translated, ostentatiously moving the Calvados, of which Angus had been allowed a small taste, out of his son's reach.

'Will you take me sometime?' Eleanor asked Angus.

'Sure,' Angus said, and blushed.

'Joe 'n' Eddie are friends of Angus,' Annie said. 'They take him out fishing with them sometimes.'

'Do you enjoy it?' Eleanor asked.

'I get sick. But I like it. They take tourists out for mackerel in the afternoons. I'll go with you, if you like.'

'Let me think about that.' Eleanor rose from the table, her robe falling in folds around her. 'Now I must go,' she said.

'I'll walk you home,' Angus said, jumping up. Her cottage was no more than two hundred yards away, but it was now silent outside.

'All right, Annie?' Eleanor asked. It was a delicate question, possibly undercutting Angus's sixteen-year-old right to make the offer by suggesting that Annie still controlled his nocturnal life, and Eleanor moved smoothly into a following remark. 'Is he just trying to get out of doing the dishes, like me?'

'Go with her, Angus,' Salter said. 'Defend her with your life. Want a gun?'

Angus had had plenty of time to shape his next fantasy. 'All I need is a bucket of water,' he said. 'It is the only thing the lava man fears.' He fetched Eleanor's cape from the hall and held it proudly while she stepped into it and gathered its folds around her. Then he went ahead of her to open the three doors and followed her out into the night.

Annie and Sheila began to clear away the dishes, while Salter tidied up the liquor bottles. Sheila smiled, apparently to herself, but held it long enough to be asked what the joke was. Now she said, 'The classical older woman syndrome. Angus is about to be seduced.'

'He's what?' Salter asked, his irritation with Annie's friend, temporarily forgotten during dinner, returning. Sheila had been with them since the beginning of their vacation and showed no signs of leaving. They had taken her in out of pity. Two days before Salter and Angus had left Toronto—to be followed later by Annie and Seth—

Sheila had called, distraught, with a request to be allowed to stay the night with the Salters. She had been assaulted by the man she lived with, an alcoholic commercial artist, who had given her a black eye. 'Why us?' Salter had asked. Sheila and Annie had been at university together and had remained in touch, but they were not close friends. 'I don't know,' Annie had said. 'Because you are a policeman? Or because she's short of friends?'

But the appeal was not to be resisted. Salter had never met Sheila, but he had seen enough battered wives to feel sorry for her, and when Annie, casting around for a way to help, had suggested they invite her to spend a few days with them on the Island, he had agreed immediately. The problem began soon after she arrived and intensified when the initial sympathy had run its course. The root of the problem lay in Sheila's new-found interest in the psychological basis of human behaviour, the result of her recently having entered analysis. Within a day of her arrival she had declared herself as someone with a special insight into human relationships and a belief in the value of laying bare her own private life as well as the necessity of speculating about everyone else's. She behaved as if there were no difference between the psychiatrist's couch and the market-place. Of Annie and Salter, on the second day of her visit, she had pointed out casually, as if commenting on the grey in his hair, that Salter was deeply dependent on Annie, which sounded bad to him. After that she found it interesting that Angus was clearly going through a period of hero-worship of his father when he ought properly to be in rebellion at this stage of his development, leaving Salter wondering what psychological torment he was laying up for his son in the future by playing golf with him now.

Twenty years before she would have seemed in possession of a special knowledge, but Sheila had come too late to her subject so that nothing she said was new or striking, and most of it had already been the subject of parody. This annoyed Salter even more because now he reacted not only with his old dislike and fear of people like her who invaded his private life, but with irritation that he was no better at flicking them off his cuff than he had ever been. The fact that she got to him at all was as annoying as what she said.

Like all enthusiasts, she was really only happy when she was talking about her enthusiasm, and she had sat silent and unsmiling for most of the time during dinner while Annie, Eleanor and Angus had talked about the books that Angus had studied in English that year and Salter drank Calvados in peace. Now, though, Sheila was free to speak, and now his irritation came back in force as he snarled at his house-guest.

'Oh, don't worry, Charlie. I meant metaphorically speaking. She won't actually drag him into bed.'

'That's good. No, that's too bad. She's a nice, sexy lady. Give him a benchmark for the future.' He was determined to outdo her, outrage her, if possible.

'Yes, it was obvious you approved of her.' They might have been discussing Eleanor's taste in clothes. 'Like father, like son.'

'That's right. I spent the evening fantasizing about what a good screw she would be.'

'And what did you conclude?'

'I didn't conclude anything. I assumed it from the start.'

Salter and Sheila spoke as if they were alone, but he was aware and reckless of Annie, with her back to them, taking longer than necessary to put cups on hooks and close the kitchen cupboards.

'Is that why you offered to teach her to play golf? After Angus takes her fishing? Eleanor the earth mother, or just mother.' All this was said in a bantering tone, not to Salter, but to the air as Sheila moved lightly from table to sink to cupboard.

Don't get into this, Salter told himself, and did. 'You

think that's what Angus is up to now? Looking to jump his mother?' Annie was now forgotten.

'That's not what I meant. But you could be right. To Angus she's friendly, motherly, and sexy. Just the one to get him through his initiation. He could trust her not to laugh at him, which is what boys of his age fear most. Fathers used to arrange these things with a friendly tart.' She was still talking to herself.

'Is that right? So what's in it for her? Do all forty-year-old women crave an adolescent lover?' he asked the back of her head.

Sheila adopted a quasi-thoughtful air. 'It must be a very uncomplicated arrangement, I should think.'

'Stop it, you two,' Annie said, still with her back to them. 'Charlie's so defensive . . .'

Annie turned to look at them. 'Both of you, and this conversation, are *off*ensive. So stop it.' She stared at both of them in turn, forcing them into silence. 'Now let's go to bed.'

Later, in bed, they went over the evening, avoiding the scene in the kitchen, but they had to come back, eventually, to Sheila.

'How did we get stuck with her?' Salter asked. 'Didn't you know what she was like?'

'No, I didn't. I made a mistake. We've had bad house-guests before. Some people are better at being guests than others.'

'She's no good at all.'

'I know. I'll look after her. All right?'

Foolishly he picked at it. 'You knew her at university, didn't you? Was she always like this?'

'Of course. I just invited her to ruin your goddamn holiday.' Annie turned and lay on her back. After a few minutes, she spoke again. 'At university she was just a nice girl from Moncton. Slightly frenetic, but nothing special. I've had lunch with her about once a month ever since she moved to Toronto. Sometimes there are four of us. We have a good time. When women get together we talk about stuff that we don't talk about when men are around. Just like you guys. Lunch-talk; woman-talk. I have a woman-talk personality you've never seen. What I thought was Sheila's woman-talk personality turned out to be the whole woman. I should have guessed, but I didn't. Now shut up about her. Stay away from her as far as you can, and don't let her get to you. Hasn't it occurred to you that some of the stuff she comes out with may be because she's uncomfortable, too? She doesn't have our kind of small-talk. Maybe for her it's the equivalent of finding herself stuck with a bunch of fundamentalists or communist-vegetarians or something. Maybe *I* gave her the wrong impression. So I'll look after her.' She turned on her side, away from him. 'She's in an embarrassing position,' she continued. 'She's not insensitive so she's certainly aware that she hasn't become one of the family. Angus alone has taken care of that, and I'm going to have to speak to him. In old-fashioned terms she realizes she is not as welcome as she expected to be, which is not a nice thing to realize. The normal reaction would be to leave as soon as possible, but perhaps she hopes that if she stays around and keeps talking we'll learn to love her. So do your best, will you? She's only been here a week, and I'm not going to ask her when she's leaving.'

'Is she coming to the wedding?' This was a union of one of Annie's second cousins with another tribe, to take place in Halifax.

'Not so far. When I told her about it she said she would stay here on her own. Now move over to your side of the bed.'

But Salter had one more question. 'Those clothes she had on tonight—are they fashionable?'

Sheila had come to dinner in a black jersey top, designed to expose one arm and a shoulder. Her skirt was white, slit open at the front so that if she sat square it fell away from her legs, and if she sat sideways, one leg and a thigh emerged. With her pale face and shiny black hair she would have turned heads in Toronto, but Salter found the effect disconcerting because it looked like a lot of work to keep the clothes from slipping off entirely. He found himself waiting for her to reach over and yank her top back over her shoulder.

'Of course they are. She looked terrific. Now shut up and go to sleep.'

CHAPTER 2

Tom Gush appeared the following Wednesday. A half-ton pick-up truck with an enclosed storage box built over the cargo space pulled up by the back fence, and Annie, busy in the kitchen, called out to Salter to pick up their order. Salter paid for the chicken and delivered the message from Eleanor. 'You've got a new customer,' he said.

'How's that?' Once Angus had christened him, it was hard not to think of him as the lava man. A dark-red, hairless head was pitted with a layer of scar tissue left behind by some skin disease, making him look as if molten rock had been poured over him and allowed to cool. His hands were the same colour and texture. He was built like a Japanese wrestler, close to the ground with a large, hard belly.

'Miss Vail. The yellow cottage down by the harbour,' Salter said.

'Oh, ah. Yes. I called on her already. Brady told me about her.' Gush seemed indisposed to chat. He turned away and climbed into his truck. 'Friend of yours, is she?' he asked, starting his engine.

'Friend of a friend.'

'Friend of Brady's?' Now Gush seemed disinclined to drive away.

'He's going to do some work for her. We put her on to him.'

'He'd have found her soon enough. By himself.'

'Brady?'

'Brady. He'd have found her soon enough.' Gush's speech came in little spurts, like jets of steam from the buried volcano his appearance suggested. 'She's a nice-looking lady who lives on her own. Brady would have found her.' There was a darker hue now underneath the red rock. Gush was getting angry, on the edge of eruption.

'He gets around, does he?' Salter asked.

'You could say that. Women. Brady gets around women.' Gush leaned out of his cab. 'That man'll get an injury done to himself one of these days. He got caught once over in Summerside without his trousers on and got himself a good hiding.'

'That bad, is he?'

Gush leaned further out. 'That man, Mr Salter, is in love with his cock,' he whispered fiercely, glancing up at the house to make sure the ladies were out of range.

'You know him pretty well, do you?'

'We're not pals, if that's what you mean, but I do know him, yes. He remodelled my truck for me, so I got to know him a bit over that. But we're not pals. He's not an Islander, you know.' Now Gush let in his clutch and made a final remark. 'That fella will get caught again without his pants on one day and that'll put an end to his games. You'll see.' He drove off, nodding.

Salter went back into the house and reported a censored version of Gush's remarks to Annie and Sheila, wondering aloud if he should say anything to Eleanor.

Annie said. 'The woman's *forty*, for God's sake. She can handle Brady.'

Salter felt foolish and changed the subject. 'Can we take one of the cars?' he asked. His inquiry was purely perfunctory because Annie and Sheila were in the middle of a full morning of house-cleaning. A few minutes later he and Angus were on their way to the golf-course.

Constable Dennis Fehely of the Cavendish detachment of the Royal Canadian Mounted Police drove off first and hit the ball smartly down the centre of the fairway. Angus followed, managing a fair hit, also staying on the fairway, but about seventy-five yards short of the Mountie. Salter wiggled his club twice and gave the ball a good blow, but catching it slightly on one side, sent it in the direction of some trees to the right of Fehely's ball. The three men organized their little carts and set off down the fairway.

'Any leads on the break-and-enter boys?' Salter asked as they walked along.

'Nothing yet, Mr Salter. We're still trying to work out a pattern. I am, anyway. My sergeant is waiting for him to make a mistake, but I'd like to catch him myself.'

'No ideas at all?'

'It's a local man,' Fehely offered.

'One guy?'

'Maybe not. Some person or persons who knows what's happening on a day-to-day basis, especially among the visitors, because in every case except one, the owner who was away for the night is a summer resident.'

'And no one has ever seen him?'

'One owner did catch a glimpse, but he couldn't identify him. He had been planning to go away but something cropped up to keep him on the Island. He heard someone at the back door and he came downstairs but whoever it was took off before he could get a good look at him.'

They had reached Angus's ball and they waited while the boy struck it another hundred yards. Then they all set off to look for Salter's ball. Fehely spotted it in the long grass between two trees.

'Shall I try for the green?' Salter asked Fehely. From the first time they had played together it was obvious that

Fehely was the expert. He had been playing since he was fourteen on the courses around Regina, where he grew up, and he expected to par most holes.

'Use a seven,' he said.

Salter changed from the five iron he had selected and took up a stance behind the ball.

'I wouldn't pull it too far left,' Fehely said courteously from behind Salter. 'You want to stay out of the water.'

Salter rearranged himself thirty degrees clockwise, struck for home, and watched the ball bounce once on the edge of a bunker and land on the green.

'Clever,' Fehely said, and walked over to his own ball.

They were all down honourably, Fehely in four, Salter in five, and Angus, who had overswiped on the green, in seven. On the way to the next tee, Salter asked, 'Could it be one of the visitors himself?'

Fehely looked surprised. 'A real amateur?'

'I'm joking, I guess. But you said he never picks the lock, just smashes his way in. Who else knows who is coming or going?'

'I figure someone like a cab-driver,' Fehely said. 'All these people took a cab to the airport, so the cabbies would know. See.'

'Did they take the same cab?'

Fehely shook his head. 'No, but these guys talk to each other, and some of them do a little bootlegging, we know that. I figure they may be in some kind of ring.'

'So what do you do next?'

'I'm making a map of the area of the break-ins. And I do a little scouting around on Saturday nights, on my own time.'

'Good luck. It's a good thing you aren't married. Does your girlfriend mind?'

'No, she wants me to get ahead. She understands. Besides, it doesn't interfere with us. I don't go out until after midnight. This guy must operate when no one is around.'

They played several more holes, concentrating on golf.

Salter counted himself lucky to have found Fehely. At a drinks party given by his in-laws he had enjoyed talking to an RCMP inspector and their chat led to a further invitation to the inspector's house in Kensington. This in turn led to a visit to the Cavendish detachment of the Mounties. Constable Fehely had been there, courteous, ambitious and calling Salter 'sir' until Salter stopped him. The inspector introduced Fehely as the police golf champion, and Salter stuck to the topic until Fehely offered to show him around the new golf-course, an offer Salter eagerly accepted.

For Salter had expected to be slightly bored, as usual, on his vacation. Prince Edward Island calls itself 'The Garden of the Gulf', which it is, a rural paradise for anyone who does not have to earn his living on the Island, and who likes the sea. It is an ideal place to retire to, or to spend a week in the summer, but after that the visitor had better find himself something to do. And this, in the past, had been Salter's problem. For one thing, Annie's family were keen sailors, but Salter, who knew nothing about sailing, had no intention of stumbling about fore and aft, being tolerated by his in-laws. When they weren't sailing they played tennis, which he didn't. His sons had taken up the Island sports from their earliest vacations, and Salter was usually left looking for someone to play golf with, or fish, his only other outdoor activity. This summer was shaping up differently, though, for Angus had decided to join his father in whatever boredom that entailed, and Salter was having a better time of it. Among its other attempts to attract tourists, the Island had created enough good and easy golf-courses to make it a haven for someone used to the crowded public courses in Toronto.

The new phase in the relationship between father and son had germinated on the long drive from Toronto. As the holidays approached, the Salters had argued about the various ways of getting to the Island and decided that Salter would drive down with Angus while Annie and Seth would fly.

They might all have flown, but Salter held out for having their own car with them in spite of the fact that Annie's father always provided them with one. Two cars gave them the freedom and mobility to go their separate ways on the Island when they felt like it. Just as important to Salter, his hidden agenda, was the pleasure he took in the prospect of spending two or three days on the road. He liked travelling and he liked driving long distances through unfamiliar country, most of the time along fairly empty highways. He liked crossing the border into the north-eastern United States—the different beer, the superior food and (he had always been lucky) the good, cheap motels. Most of all he liked one good car-trip a year, preferably with Annie and no kids, but alone was pretty good, too, because then he could start the day at five o'clock if he woke up at sparrowfart in a motel in the Maine north woods. In the States, in the small towns, people wake at dawn and go out for breakfast, because there is always a diner open, whereas in Canada he had once driven along the Nova Scotia shore from Lunenberg to Halifax for an hour in the early morning until finally at eight o'clock he had found someone willing to sell him a cup of coffee. It was a favourite speculation as to why this difference should be. Did all maritime Canadians eat at home? Did most Americans not? Did that explain the plethora of seafood restaurants along the Maine coast, an abundance which stopped dead at the Canadian border?

He proposed therefore that he should take the heavy luggage in the family car and leave three days early, and be in time to meet Annie and the boys at the airport in Charlottetown.

Angus said, 'I'll come with you, Dad.'

Surprise, pleasure and disappointment jostled each other inside Salter when he heard this suggestion. Why did Angus want to come with him? It was nice that he wanted to, but how would the boy/man be as a travelling companion? Apart from other, more selfish, reactions, Salter felt a sprouting fear of the responsibility the offer placed on him. Would he be able to keep the kid happy and interested for three days?

'Terrific,' he said.

'Could I get my licence before we go?'

Ah-ha. 'Sure. That would be a great idea,' Salter said, fairly certain that it wouldn't happen in time.

But Angus was seized with the project, and applied most of his savings and all of his spare time to it, passing his test on the first try with a week to spare. So they set off at six o'clock in the morning with Salter driving, arrived in Montreal by noon and at two o'clock they were parked across the Vermont border eating lunch. 'Now,' Salter said. 'You drive.'

And he did, neatly and carefully, causing Salter afterwards to watch his own driving habits when Angus was in the car. He took them all the way to Bangor and they did the first six hundred miles in one day, breaking all previous records.

The trip was a delight. They said very little during the morning of the first day as Salter settled in to enjoy himself and Angus watched him drive and made occasional remarks about the way others were driving. Late in the afternoon, after Angus was well into his first long stint behind the wheel, the subject of driving and the road lost its interest, and the car turned into a space capsule in which they were alone in the universe. Angus said, 'Why don't you ever give me any advice, Dad?'

'What do you want me to tell you? You're driving fine.' Salter's legs ached, his crotch was binding no matter how he sat, and his throat was bone dry, but they had come five hundred miles and he was looking forward to his first draught Michelob completely at peace with the world.

'Not about driving. About anything.'

Hullo, thought Salter. What's this all about. 'Like what?' Death? Sex? Politics? 'What do you want to know?'

'About life and stuff. What I should do. You know.'

'No, I don't. Do you mean like "Don't steal caviar from the supermarket"?'

'No, that's a *rule*. The other kids at school get all kinds of *advice* from their parents. I don't.'

'Like what?' Salter was curious now. 'Give me an example.'

'John Purbrick's father told him never to borrow or lend money.'

'That's bullshit. Give me another.'

'Never pick up hitch-hikers.'

'That's good advice. You know why?'

'Because they might be dangerous.'

'No. Because they might be boring. I picked up a guy once going from Montreal to Rivière du Loup who spent the whole trip telling me what foods to eat to keep my blood clear. Give me another piece of advice.'

'You being serious?'

'Sure I am. Give me another one.'

'Paul Clemas's dad says you should never bring out your wallet in public when you're travelling.

'What does Clemas's dad do when the bill comes? Go into the can to get the right change?'

'I think he means you shouldn't flash your money around.'

'I'm sure he does. Any more?'

'Yeah, there's lots. I can't think of any right now. But you never give me any.'

'You want me to start? Okay. Never fight fair with a stranger.'

'That's a quote.'

'Okay. Never draw to an inside straight.'

'What's that mean?'

Salter explained. 'And try this: "Better stay silent and be thought a fool than open your mouth and remove all doubt."'

'That's *another* quote.'

'I'm just practising. Anyway, you think your friends' fathers make up their own? Except Clemas's dad, maybe. He sounds pretty original. Probably rich, too. All right, I'll come clean. I don't give advice to you because I don't have any. I don't know what made me the amazing success I am. Not following a bunch of advice, not my own, anyway. I just fumble along on luck and instinct, I guess. I don't know how to tell you to have a good life. Win a lottery, work hard, find a nice girl. All I can tell you is, don't let anyone advise you to do anything you don't want to do. Trust your instincts. If you like someone, then lend them money if they ask for it, but don't count on getting it back or you might spend years blaming yourself for not listening to Purbrick's father. Let's change that around a bit: never lend more money than you can afford, and then don't lend it, give it. It'll probably come back. There. That's all I've learned about money and it probably only works for me, which is the trouble with advice. You'll have to find out about women for yourself; all advice about women is useless. As to a career, you want to be an actor, right? I have no idea if that's a good thing to want, but go ahead. What do I know about actors, except that most of them are out of work? Sorry. That sounds like a warning, a piece of advice. It isn't. I don't have any advice about acting.'

Angus was silent. Salter continued, 'But you've got me going now. I'm going to spend the next two days thinking up advice.'

A town came into view and Salter told Angus to slow down. 'See that motel sign?' he intoned pompously. 'Never stay at a motel called the OKUM INN. The owner spent so much energy thinking up the name he has none left over to run the place.'

Angus laughed. 'What about that?' Attached to the motel was a restaurant, 'Mary's Home-Cooked Meals.'

'An absolute no-no. Never eat at "Mary's Home-Cooked

Meals", because by the time she gets the food from her home to the restaurant it's stone cold. We'll have a beer there, though. Then let's see if we can make Bangor.'

In Bangor, Salter rejected the first motel they stopped at ('Never stay at a two-storey motel made of logs. They cost a fortune,') in favour of a comfortable-looking establishment on the edge of town, a motel which triggered no negative advice, and had a coffee-shop that opened at six. For the next twenty-four hours Salter kept it up, inventing absurd maxims that occasionally made sense, and Angus contributed some of his own. His best was, 'Never eat at a restaurant that advertises "Canadians Welcome". The specialty of the house will be chips and gravy.'

They left Bangor at seven, keen to make the Island in record time, and arrived at Cape Tormentine at two in the afternoon. There was the usual line-up for the ferry, but Salter accepted the wait as the necessary price of doing without the causeway that was being forever planned. Salter had a romantic streak; he liked ferries, liked arriving at an island by boat.

They debated whether to call in on Annie's parents in Charlottetown first, but the salt air was in their lungs now, and both of them were keen to see the cottage, so they headed directly across the Island. Prince Edward Island is Canada's smallest province and in summer its two-coloured landscape of green and red makes it the prettiest. The ironstone which colours the soil is so distinctive that gas station attendants in Montreal, six hundred miles away, can identify a car from the island by the red dust on its wheels. Angus drove carefully from the ferry docks onto the imposing piece of highway, complete with cloverleaf and multi-directional overhead signs, which turns almost immediately, like a false storefront, into a comfortable two-lane road through the fields and brightly painted villages of Green Gables' country, as domesticated as the English countryside, but with the slightly toyland quality given it by the coloured wooden houses. They arrived at the cottage in an hour and collected the key from the woman next door before setting out to look for a hamburger.

The trip had linked the two of them together, and when the holiday began Angus attached himself to Salter, eschewing sailing and tennis. Salter began to teach the boy to play golf, a game Angus took to with a passion, and now, with Constable Fehely, Salter had just the right mix for teaching Angus and improving his own game.

Salter found Fehely slightly touching. He had been in the RCMP for only a year, and this was his first posting. They played golf twice a week after their first day, talking shop continually. Fehely was extremely keen to get ahead, and avid for stories about police work. For Salter it had been a bargain; he got the services of a pro for him and Angus all for the price of a bit of chat about life in the Toronto police. Angus, too, was enjoying learning to play under Fehely's eye, and enjoying with pride the deference with which Fehely treated his father.

On the eighteenth hole, Fehely said, 'What do you think, Mr Salter?'

'Charlie,' Salter reminded him. 'I'm not your boss. About what?'

'About my idea. That it could be a gang of cab-drivers.'

Not much, thought Salter. While waiting for Annie and Seth to arrive from Toronto he had noticed a passenger from another flight looking for a cab at the airport. There were two empty cabs standing outside the door of the airport lounge and, as Salter watched, the man had gone back and forth a number of times looking for the drivers. Eventually a freckled lad sitting by the door admitted that yes, he was a cab-driver, and yes, he was hoping for a fare. He was the only shy cab-driver Salter had ever encountered, an unlikely candidate to be part of a ring of thieves. 'I guess it could be something like that,' he said. 'But keep an open mind. Sometimes the only connection

in a string of break-ins is that after the first couple of robberies someone else gets the same idea, so don't eliminate
anyone just because he wasn't around for one of the break-
ins.'

'But I think it has to be something like that, someone who
knows when people are away.'

'They don't take any TVs or stereos, you say?'

'No. Just money and jewellery.'

'They would be very hard to catch with the stuff on them.
Are there any fences on the Island?'

'A couple, but mostly they deal in what people need. Like,
you want a stereo, then you go to this guy and he arranges
to have it lifted and he charges you three times what he
gives the thieves, but you still get a bargain. We're watching
them, but nothing has turned up yet.'

'Have you tried Montreal or Toronto?'

'Sure. We've put the stuff that can be identified on the
CPI computer, but we don't have much hope.'

They had reached their cars now, and Angus had put the
golf-bags in the back and was waiting to go. 'I think your
sergeant's right,' Salter said. 'You'll have to catch him in
the act. Same time Monday?'

'Sure.' Fehely nodded to Angus. 'Two weeks, Angus, and
you'll be able to beat your old man.'

Angus writhed with pleasure. 'Naah,' he said. 'Anyway,
it's you I want to beat.'

Driving home, Angus asked, 'Would it bother you if I
beat you, Dad?'

'I'd cry my eyes out, but I'd get over it. What makes you
say that?'

'Something Sheila said.'

'What? What did she say?'

'I couldn't get it all. Something about the problem men
had when their drive weakens. But you can still hit pretty
good, can't you?'

I'll kill her, Salter thought first; and then: Is this kid

putting me on? He looked sharply at Angus. No. 'Who was she talking to, your mother?' he asked.

'Yes, this morning before we left.'

'With you there?'

'No, I interrupted them. Mum said, 'Oh, and when does that start to happen?' and then they saw me.'

Salter smiled. 'Sheila doesn't know a goddamn thing about golf, does she?'

'I guess not. Does Mum?'

Fortunately they were turning into the garage, and Salter had no more need to answer. He did, though, after he had had time to think. 'She's picked up a lot from hearing me talk. Leave the bags in the car. We'll take them out if anyone needs the space before Monday.'

CHAPTER 3

But that was the last game Salter and Fehely played for some time. On Sunday morning, while the Salter household was enjoying a ritual brunch of finnan haddie, the Mountie appeared at the house. Angus answered the door and brought him into the kitchen where they were eating.

'I'm just on my way back to the detachment,' he said to Salter, after acknowledging Annie and Sheila. 'I called in to say we won't be playing golf for a bit.'

'Have some coffee,' Annie said. 'Angus, get Mr Fehely a chair.'

'Thanks.' Fehely sat down and looked for somewhere to put his hat, eventually balancing it on his knee. 'Been a bad incident,' he began.

'Another robbery?'

'Worse than that. A homicide.'

'Here? In Marlow?' Annie was shocked.

Fehely nodded. 'A man named Clive Elton was killed last

night. Joe Pethwick was on patrol and he saw the lights on and the door open when he was passing, about five o'clock this morning. Mr Elton was in the kitchen. It looks like he disturbed someone trying to rob him.' Fehely focused on Salter, trying to make his news something matter-of-fact between policemen, but he was obviously full of it. Salter guessed that it was Fehely's first homicide, and certainly his first on the Island.

'Did you get any sleep last night?' he asked Fehely.

'Oh yes. I was in bed by twelve and I wasn't disturbed until Joe came for me at six.'

'Dennis had been trying to catch the guy who's been robbing the houses around here.' Salter explained to the others.

'I would have missed him anyway,' Fehely said. 'I was planning to take a look up by Dalvay. Mr Dougan said he was going to be away and we told him we'd keep an eye on the house. I thought I might get lucky but I fell asleep and never went out. I wasn't on duty, of course.'

'Is everything finished at Elton's house?'

'Just about. They've taken him away and the technical people are nearly through.

Annie refilled his cup. 'Did you say Elton? Clive Elton?'

Fehely nodded. 'A schoolteacher. Lived in the grey house near the end of the point.'

'Was he married? Is his wife all right? Is there anything I can do?'

Fehely shook his head. 'He was a bachelor. Lived by himself. He did have a girlfriend. She lives in Marlow.'

'The poor girl. Is she all right?'

'She's got some friends with her, I think.'

Annie put the coffee-pot down on the stove. 'Elton,' she repeated. 'I think Daddy knows him. I think they've been involved together in something lately. He's a historian of some kind, isn't he?'

'According to his girlfriend, he's been doing some part-time work for the government. I don't know exactly what.'

'Mum and Dad are coming for lunch. I wonder if he's heard?'

'By lunch-time the whole Island will know,' Salter said.

'Do you have any leads, Constable?' Sheila asked.

'If he does, he won't be telling us.'

Fehely, who'd been about to speak, closed his mouth and stood up. 'Time to go.' He had relaxed somewhat over his coffee. Now he looked like a policeman investigating your average homicide. 'Take your dad out for a game, Angus. I'll be with you in a week or so.'

'Angus might have killed him by then,' Sheila said.

Fehely looked from her to Salter, to Angus, and back to Salter.

'It's a family joke,' Salter said. He showed Fehely to the front door. When they were away from the kitchen, he said, 'What did they find? Was he shot?'

'No. Clobbered with a bar or something. His forehead was crushed in.'

'When?'

'The doctor reckons he'd been dead for about two hours. That would make it about three o'clock.'

'Thanks for calling in. We'll see you when you're free. Lotsa luck.'

When he returned to the kitchen, Annie and Sheila were silently clearing away the dishes.

'I think I puzzled your young Mountie,' Sheila said.

'Probably. And I don't know what the hell you were talking about, either.'

'I was speaking mythically, of course.'

'Of course. I'll explain it to him when he hasn't got a homicide on his mind.' He stood up. 'I'm going to town to see if there's somewhere I can buy yesterday's *Globe.*'

'I'll come with you,' Angus said, putting down the dish-towel he had picked up in a half-hearted attempt to help the women.

In the car, he asked, 'What was Sheila really talking about, Dad?'

'Don't ask me. And don't ask her, either. Maybe she'll stop talking if no one encourages her.' It was unfair, setting up a conspiracy with a sixteen-year-old, and from the look on Angus's face he was pleased, but Salter felt that making Angus his buddy relieved slightly his desire to tip over his house-guest's chair the next time she analysed his world.

In Charlottetown it looked as though there had been a run on the *Globe and Mail* because all the street boxes were empty. They found a store open and Salter asked the owner if he still had a *Globe* left.

'Sure,' the man said, with a round-faced grin, and disappeared into the back of the shop, reappearing with a small globe. 'This do?' he asked.

Another customer, waiting his turn to be served, chuckled. 'Old Hector is a real character,' he said.

'I mean a *Globe and Mail*,' Salter said. 'The paper.'

'Oh. You said "Globe", didn't he, Fred? I thought you meant one of these.' He looked long at Fred, grinning.

Salter waited a patient interval, then asked, 'Do you sell the Toronto *Globe and Mail*?'

Quick as a flash, the man said, 'I have to, don't I? I used to give them away, but my wife objected.' This time he invited Angus to share his glee, and Angus managed a faint smile. Eventually Salter got his paper and they left the store.

Angus, still not certain of what his proper reaction ought to be, said, 'I guess he's a character all right, eh, Dad?'

Several things came together in Salter's mind. 'You've got it, son. That's what he is, what people call a real character. So let me give you a piece of advice. Whenever someone tells you that so-and-so is a real character, avoid him like he's got smallpox. Because nine times out of ten, what people mean when they say someone's a character is that he's an asshole, doing a number. So when you hear

"quite a character" substitute "asshole". Tell your pal
Clemas that.'

Salter felt better after that but still not keen to hurry back
to Sheila Tupper so he drove by a circuitous route that took
in part of Kings County. When he got back, Annie's parents
had already arrived, and his father-in-law was waiting to
tell him some news. Salter hid his paper so that it wouldn't
be used for wrapping garbage before he had read it, and
followed the old man out on to the porch.

Annie's father was a doctor turned businessman and,
now, backroom politician, one of the chief bagmen for the
party in power on the Island. He had come to politics too
late for a career in office, but he was enjoying himself hugely
in an unpaid but influential role. A large, ebullient man, he
was on good terms with everyone from the mailman to the
Premier. He had been a successful doctor, but when he
took over the family businesses on the death of Annie's
grandfather, he had found them more interesting than medi-
cine and closed his practice except for half a dozen very old
patients who believed he was a magician and refused to be
abandoned. Now he had discovered politics and was rapidly
becoming absorbed by it, leaving the businesses to his two
sons to look after.

Salter got along with his father-in-law but he had no sort
of relationship with him. From the beginning he had resisted
being integrated into the Montagu clan; he felt his working-
class background when he was among them, and without
being prickly he maintained a distance from them to keep
their assumption—that he was one of them—in check. The
thousand miles that normally separated their worlds made
this easy, but on the annual trip to the Island his fundamen-
tal wariness resurfaced. Once, during a very bad patch in
his career, the suggestion had come to him through Annie,
who should have known better, that he would be welcome
to join the family enterprises on the Island, and the violence

of his reaction had shown him as well as Annie how close
to the surface his wariness lay.

In spite of this, or because of it, he was on good terms
with his in-laws—courteous, friendly, but never intimate.
They made him welcome, and since their table-manners
were not so different from his own, he was able to enjoy
their company for long periods at a stretch.

Now Salter poured some beer and closed the door, wondering what he was going to hear.

'You've lost all your money and you're coming to live
with us in Toronto,' he prompted. 'Fine. I'll get the base-
ment fixed up for you. Put in a bathroom.'

'I'd harvest Irish moss before I'd live in Toronto. No, it's
about the man who was killed last night. Clive Elton.'

'Annie said you knew him. I'm sorry. Was he a friend?'

'What? Oh no. I knew him, yes. We've been working on
a scheme together for the last few weeks.'

'Doing what?'

'He was just about to bring the Great Silver Seal back to
the Island.'

Salter blinked, confused. He had been ready to go through
the motions of sympathy about the death of Elton, but
Montagu was looking at him excitedly as he waited for
Salter to react. There was no hint of grief. Salter took a sip
of his beer. 'That sounds like one of Angus's fantasies. What
is the Great Silver Seal? The Moby Dick of Prince Edward
Island? The big one you only see by moonlight?'

'Not that kind of seal.' Montagu dropped his slightly
portentous manner, and continued. 'A seal is—you know I
don't *know* what a seal is. It's what people used to make
their own mark in sealing wax with. A provincial seal must
be what the Lieutenant-Governor used to stamp laws with,
make them legal. Anyway, Prince Edward Island once had
a great seal, a silver one, an official one, the Great Silver
Seal. It disappeared during the American War of Independence. An American ship which was supposed to be blockad-

ing the Island—stopping supplies from England from being landed—came into Charlottetown and did a certain amount of looting, and in the course of it they made off with the seal. They were mercenaries really, I guess; anyway they acted like pirates. George Washington apologized for their behaviour afterwards because he had issued instructions that they were not to interfere with the settlements.

'The ship came from Marblehead in Massachussetts and when they returned home they were severely reprimanded but the loot was never recovered. It has always been assumed that the seal was either melted down or was still lying about Marblehead somewhere, probably in some attic. Until a few weeks ago. Now it's turned up.' Montagu stood up and checked that the door was closed.

'On the Island?'

'No, where you would expect, in Marblehead. Apparently a private collector down there discovered it in a job lot he bought in an estate sale. He knew enough to identify it as Canadian, and he got in touch with a dealer in Toronto who recognized the emblem of the Island—you know, the oak tree sheltering the three little trees—did a little reading on the subject and guessed that what the collector had was the missing seal. This dealer confirmed the description and asked for some pictures to be taken. They kept the whole thing quiet until they were sure. In the meantime the man in Marblehead had some tests done to prove that the thing was made of eighteenth-century silver. Apparently each age has mixed different things in to make silver workable and you can tell by assaying it when a silver object was cast or moulded or whatever the term is. That, together with the picture, was pretty conclusive, so the dealer got in touch with us and asked if we wanted to buy it.'

'Who is "us"?'

'The government,' Montagu said, surprised. 'Well, the party really.' He grinned knowingly.

The party, Salter thought. We've never talked politics.

Does he know I wouldn't vote for his party if they offered to make me chief of police?

'So how did Elton get involved?' he asked.

'He's an antiquarian. Is that the term? A local historian. Does a lot of work for the Heritage foundation. He's a man anyone would go to to check out something like this. I think he had made a bit of a name for himself. Why?'

'Somebody killed the guy.' In case anyone's interested.

'I don't think the seal has anything to do with that. It seems obvious enough that poor Clive got in the way of a local thug.'

'I guess so. So what happened? Why didn't you buy this seal?'

'Oh, we did. Or we agreed to. Three of us got together to find the money and present the seal to the government.'

'Who are "us" now?'

'Call us Friends of the Island. Two or three local business-men. Don't be naïve, Charlie. Call us the little green machine.'

'Why couldn't the government just buy it? Why do you backstage boys have to get into the act?'

'Normally that's what the government would do. But we wanted to keep it private for a while, and that's difficult if you go about it officially. There's bound to be someone who isn't—what's the phrase those silly buggers in Ottawa use these days?—"politically astute", that's it, some aide who would tell the story around the yacht club, and we'd lose our advantage.'

'Of what? You'd still have the seal.'

'There's an election coming up, and timing might be helpful. We thought of announcing the find about a week before the vote. You know, "Government Recovers Island Heritage". We were going to give the press a bit of a cloak-and-dagger story about how a secret government team had been on the track of the seal for months and finally managed to recover it—at no cost to the taxpayer, because a group of patriotic citizens had agreed to find the money and present the seal to the Island. Politicians have been elected on less, especially around here.'

Island politics, as Salter understood them from Montagu, were simple in the extreme. Anyone who wished to study the workings of patronage would find the Island an excellent laboratory without any of the elaborations and complications necessitated by the size of the federal pork-barrel. 'It's like starting with a Brownie box camera if you want to understand the principles of photography,' Montagu said. The Island government had no fat jobs to offer, no seats on the board of Air Canada or juicy diplomatic posts in London or Paris. What it had was roads and winter employment. If a Liberal government was elected, then ridings which had voted Liberal could count on getting some roads fixed. Those that voted Conservative had to wait for the next election. The jobs that changed hands were mostly menial, snow-plough operators, for example, but very welcome to the hard-up farmers who voted correctly.

'How much is involved?' Salter asked.

'What? Oh, twenty thousand dollars.'

'Is that a fair price?'

'Who knows? The thing is priceless, but the farther away you get from the Island the more it becomes just a curiosity. For someone in Texas, the Great Silver Seal would be on a par with a watch-fob found in the Alamo.'

'So why did this guy in Marblehead agree to sell and how did you fix a price? Why didn't he ask half a million?'

'We couldn't have raised half a million. That's about four dollars a head for the entire population. And the collector had a problem. The seal is worth a lot here on the Island, but if he tried to sell it to us publicly, he might run up against our laws, our right to take possession of historical artifacts, especially if they had been stolen from us in the first place. We might ask the Federal government to intervene. Like the Elgin marbles. I doubt if we would have got anywhere, but I think it gave him pause, made him play it safe. As soon as it crossed the border we could bring an action to seize it, maybe. So his potential buyers would be restricted to Americans with a curiosity interest in the thing. It isn't a work of art, after all. I think it worked. Elton did a good job for us; we fixed a price and made a deal. We were afraid that the seal would disappear into someone's private collection for another two hundred years.'

'But if the thing really belonged to the Island, couldn't you, in fact, have got the Pentagon or whoever it is to lean on the guy a little and give it back?'

'You're missing the point, Charlie. Everyone, including the collector, had thought of that, and everything else you are about to think up. I simplified the story to you a bit. In his original approach to the dealer in Toronto, the man from Marblehead was careful to say that he, personally, was not in possession of the seal, but he knew where it was to be found, and *his* client insisted on absolute anonymity, as he did himself. Apparently that's allowed in art circles. So if we'd made any gestures like that the seal would have disappeared. A bit like a kidnapper threatening to kill his victim if there's any funny business.

'You sure the whole thing wasn't a scam? It sounds fishy as hell.'

'On whose part? Remember we had the word of the owner that the thing was made of eighteenth-century silver. We had pictures of it that Elton could verify. We did ask that Elton be allowed to see the thing in Marblehead, but the owner said no. He didn't see how he could protect his identity. So we said that we would pay only after we had received the seal, and had it authenticated by Elton. The Toronto man put his reputation on the line with his client, guaranteed him there would be no funny business once we got our hands on the seal, and the Marblehead man agreed to deliver the seal to Toronto. We said further that if the seal later turned out to be fake, we wanted a guarantee that the Toronto man would refund our money, and he agreed. Presumably he got the same guarantee from his client. What I've learned from all this is that art dealers routinely swindle each other if they can, but once a deal is set that involves their reputation, then their word is their bond. At any rate we were completely protected whether the seal was authentic or not, and there wasn't all that much money involved.'

'So what happens now? You have to start again? Get someone else to represent you? Where's the seal now?'

'In Toronto, I guess. Elton was supposed to have made the arrangements on Friday, when he went to Toronto, and he was going back this week to pick it up. The Premier was going to unveil the story at a press conference about two days before the election. We are still in the same position, but we need someone else to pick it up. I talked to the others this morning when I heard the news, and we agreed that nothing's changed, but we need a courier to go to Toronto, someone who can keep his mouth shut. So here's the pitch, Charlie. Would you mind? I'd go myself, but I've given up flying, and it's one hell of a train trip, about five days there and back. I thought you might enjoy it.'

Without Fehely to play with, Salter saw some quiet days ahead. 'Okay,' he said. 'When?'

'I'm not sure. Elton managed everything by phone, so I'll call the Toronto dealer tomorrow and fix a date and time. Thanks. Poor old Clive. He was as excited by this thing as a stamp collector finding a Penny Black. He would have been a celebrity when the story came out. Internationally famous—well, around here anyway. We're still in business, though, as far as the election is concerned.'

'Without Elton, how are you going to authenticate this thing when I bring it back?'

'We'll have to trust the Toronto man. Remember we aren't paying him until we are sure, but the money isn't the main thing. We don't want egg on our face afterwards. If it is—what was the word? a scam?—then it could backfire.

But I don't see how it could be, do you? We'll establish that it wasn't stolen, although the Toronto dealer has guaranteed us against that, too. We'll find another expert to give his two cents' worth, just to make sure, then we'll let the Historical Board have a look—swear them to secrecy, they'll love it. Then we'll go ahead.'

'So when will I know?'

'I'll call you tomorrow, after I've spoken to the dealer. Keep it close, Charlie. Tell Annie, of course, so that she doesn't think you're going to Toronto to see your popsie, but no one else. Even Annie's mother doesn't know.'

Not, Salter thought, because of any security risk, but because you are enjoying yourself too much. 'Okay, I'll tell her I'm being sent on a secret mission, by agents of the government. You. She'll laugh her head off.'

'Who will?' Sheila asked, appearing on the porch, followed by Annie and her mother.

'You will,' Salter said. 'Robert just told me a good story, unsuitable for mixed company, so I'll tell Annie and she can tell you.'

'Leave me out,' Mrs Montagu said. 'I never get dirty jokes.'

'They are mostly a way of uncapping what is normally repressed,' Sheila said. 'If you are afraid of women, you tell dirty jokes. Racist jokes come from wanting to put down other kinds of people we feel threatened by.'

'This one will stand your hair on end,' Salter said. 'It's about a gay dwarf.'

'What oft was thought but ne'er so well expressed,' Mrs Montagu murmured, quoting verse, as was her habit from her days as a high school teacher of English. 'Lunch will be ready in half an hour. Why don't you men get us a drink?'

CHAPTER 4

But when the call came from Montagu the next morning, Salter's trip was cancelled. On being informed of Elton's death, the dealer had reacted by asking, 'Is the seal gone? Did they get it?' He had then gone on to tell Montagu that Elton had picked up the seal on Saturday and brought it back to the Island. If it wasn't in the house, then the killer must have it. He decided on the spot to fly down immediately and meet with Annie's father. He would arrive on the afternoon plane and be at Montagu's house by three.

'Why? Why did Elton bring the seal back? I thought he was supposed to pick it up this week?' Salter asked.

'Callendar, the dealer, said they were worried about security. They thought that someone might know that Elton was going to Toronto next week to pick up something valuable. I think they meant me—that I would blab it all over the Island. Anyway they were afraid some crook would waylay Elton and steal the thing so they decided it would be smart for Elton to bring it back now.'

Salter took the phone away from his ear and stared at it in disbelief. When he replaced it, Montagu was saying, 'Charlie, Charlie? Are you still there?'

'Yeah, yeah, I'm here. How well did you know Elton? Did he read a lot of thrillers?'

'What?'

'Elton. Did he read thrillers? Espionage stuff?'

'Why?'

'Well, frankly, off the top of my head, I never heard such a load of bullshit in my life. Some kind of conspiracy to heist the Great Silver Seal, for God's sake? You sure he wasn't putting you on?'

'I don't know. I think Callendar could be right.' Montagu sounded offended.

'Come on, Robert. The thing isn't worth peanuts except to your little gang. You told me that yourself.'

'Well, that's what Callendar said.'

And you believed him, Salter thought. He began to get some idea of the size of political coup that Montagu thought he was pulling off, and realizing this, saw also that if Elton had been similarly consumed, then he, too, might have believed it. It depended on your perspective. But Callendar, on the other hand, was a major Toronto dealer. His commission on the deal would not have paid his monthly rent. 'Can I come over and meet this guy?' he asked.

'I wish you would.' Now Montagu sounded uncertain of himself, glad of Salter's help. 'I'll let the police know,' he said.

'Let me do that,' Salter said quickly. 'Do you have a picture of the seal?'

'No, Elton had the picture, so I suppose it's still in the house. Would you ask the police not to publicize it until we've had a chance to think?'

'I'll *ask* them, Robert. I won't *tell* them, though. They'll do what they think best.'

Salter set off for the police station with a light heart. This was a whole lot better than the farm auction he had been planning to go to with Annie and Sheila.

At the Cavendish police detachment he found Fehely and told his story.

'They've put together a team to investigate the homicide,' Fehely said. 'Staff Sergeant Croll is in charge. He's here now. I'll take you in to him.'

A large man with grey wavy hair sat behind his desk watching them as they came into the room. He waited until Fehely had announced Salter, and then until Fehely had left, shutting the door after him. 'You're the Toronto guy that Fehely plays golf with,' he said. 'We met once, didn't we?'

'That's right. Charlie Salter. I called in once, too, but you were out.'

Croll waited a few more moments, then stood up and put out his hand. 'Brian Croll. Take a seat. What can I do for you? I thought you were on holiday.'

'I am. I'm a messenger boy today, though.'

The pace of Croll's response to Salter's appearance had put the Mountie in charge, and Salter waited to be told to continue.

'What's the message?' Croll asked.

'Robert Montagu is my wife's father,' Salter began.

'I know.'

'He said he'd met you.'

Croll nodded.

'He has an interest in Clive Elton's death,' Salter said.

'What kind of interest?'

'He thinks Elton may have had something in his possession when he was killed. Something that belongs or should belong to the government.'

'Montagu isn't in the government, is he?'

'No, but he's been advising the Premier about this thing.'

'I adwise the crew,' Croll said.

'Sorry?'

'A private joke. I took a trip to Europe once and came back on that Russian ship, the *Alexander Pushkin*. There was this character on board who just hung around, a guy about our age in a black suit and a greasy black tie. The only thing he did was hand out table-tennis balls if anyone wanted to play, and collect them at the end of the game. Otherwise he was just there. After about four days an Australian on board got a little tanked up and asked him who the hell he was. "I adwise the crew," the guy said. That's all. I always think of him when someone is called an adviser.'

'This is just Island politics. I don't think my father-in-law is connected to the KGB.'

'But he does adwise the Premier.'

'Sure, but . . . Look, let me tell you what this thing is all about, eh?'

'Go ahead. Want some coffee?'

Salter shook his head and began his story. Croll heard him out, then added up the essential points.

'So this seal was in the house when Elton was robbed, right?'

'That's what the dealer thinks.'

'So if it's not there now, the killer has it. Right?'

'Unless the dealer is lying.'

Croll nodded. 'Good point. Assume everyone's lying. What about your father-in-law?'

'He's not lying.'

Croll laughed. 'No, I guess not. Not to you, anyway. No, what I meant was, he still thinks he might be able to go ahead if we find this thing for him. That's why he doesn't want any publicity.'

'That's right. It's a big deal for him.'

'We've got one problem. We don't know what is missing. Elton was a bachelor, with no relatives living in the house. We're going to have to ask around to see who knew what he had that might be missing. There's a lot of stuff that a regular thief would have taken, including some money in a drawer in the bedroom—why do people do that?—so it looks to us as if the thief was disturbed before he finished. He just clobbered Elton and ran. There's a girlfriend, a schoolteacher Elton was seeing. He was with her that night. She's going over the house this morning to see if she can spot anything missing. It might be that the killer didn't take *anything*. Did this Toronto dealer know Elton well?'

'I don't think so. They only came together because of the seal.'

Croll spread his hands on the desk. 'What are you up to now, Salter?'

'How do you mean?'

'Now. Right now. You can't play golf with Fehely. I need him until this thing's cleared up. Why don't you come over to Elton's house with me? We'll have a look around. All the experts are finished. Maybe we'll find this great seal in a cupboard. What does it look like?'

'Montagu said there is a picture of it around. He's seen one but Elton kept the copies which the dealer sent him. They are probably in his house.'

'Let's have a look.'

It suited Salter's mood and interest exactly. 'Then maybe you should come back and meet the dealer. He'll be at my father-in-law's this afternoon.'

Croll nodded. 'Let's go, then.'

They took the Mountie's car and drove back to Marlow. At the door of Elton's cottage a constable was watching out for them and he took them through to the kitchen.

'There is where they found him,' Croll said. 'The light was on and the door was open. The killer probably had a car parked behind the hedge, though we haven't found any tracks.'

Salter looked around. Clive Elton, he had learned from his father-in-law, was an Islander by birth who had been raised by his aunt in Summerside after his parents died. Elton had graduated in history from Dalhousie and gone to Toronto to take his MA. He had worked as a history teacher in several schools in southern Ontario, coming back to the Island very rarely to see his aunt and the one or two people he still knew. But when his aunt died she had left him a house and several mortgages she owned, and Elton had by now twenty years in the Ontario Secondary Schools' pension fund, so he took a deferred pension to take care of his old age and retired to the Island, trading in the house in Summerside for a cottage and a little money to add to the income from the mortgages to enable him to subsist. He worked as a supply teacher on the Island for a couple of years, joined the party in power, and made himself useful enough as a volunteer to be worth paying as a minor functionary. His ambition, soon to be realized, was a regular job with the civil service in the provincial archives offices, where he would have been happy for the rest of his life, for Elton's passion had become local history, and he had become a collector of Island memorabilia.

The kitchen reflected Elton's interests and his modest income. It was neither carefully restored nor particularly modern, even by Island standards. It was just the kitchen of a not-very-well-off bachelor, although there were a few objects—an ancient rocking-chair, a huge ironstone serving dish in the shape of a fish, an old framed photograph of one of the first Island ferries, the *Abegweit*, that showed Elton's interests.

The living-room, too, was a muddle of practical furniture —one of the armchairs was a Lay-Z-Boy—and some older pieces that had obviously been collected. There were two desks: one, Elton's working desk, a huge ugly object in light oak with a lot of drawers and a giant superstructure of shelves and pigeonholes; the other was a small battered antique pine desk, probably a schoolteacher's, with a rail along the back from which a spindle was missing.

'This is what I mean.' Croll picked up a silver desk set from the pine desk. 'My guess is that this is an antique worth money. He didn't take everything. That camera looks to be worth a few dollars, too. Come upstairs.'

In the main bedroom, opposite Elton's bed, which had been roughly made up, there was a nondescript bureau. 'We found a couple of hundred dollars, his passport, an old watch and a bit of jewellery, cufflinks and the like, all in the drawer here. The first place a real thief would look.'

'No sign of the seal, though,' Salter said.

'Let's have a good look round.'

They did a thorough search of the house, covering all the hiding-places dear to householders, and came up empty-handed. Going through the oak desk, Salter found the photographs of the seal. There were six of them, three of each side of the seal, part of a bundle of prints tucked away in a paper folder of the kind that photographic printers use for their customers. The pictures were in black and white.

'Where did they come from?' Cross asked. 'Who took them?'

'The guy who owns the seal in Massachusetts. Montagu told me that it was on the basis of these pictures that Elton could confirm that the seal was probably authentic.'

'Has anyone seen the seal? Anyone on the Island?'

'Only Elton, and according to the dealer he only saw it for the first time on Saturday.'

Croll started to put the pictures in his wallet.

'You need all those copies?' Salter asked.

Croll selected one of each and handed the rest to Salter. 'You want to show Montagu?'

'Yeah. He might need them if this becomes news, as it's bound to, I guess.'

Croll nodded. 'What time do you meet this dealer?'

'Three o'clock. You coming?'

'Oh yes. I have a lot of questions to ask about this seal, don't I? How big was it? How was it wrapped? When did Elton pick it up? You know.'

'You want to have a sandwich first?'

'Sure. Let's go to the coffee-shop down the street.'

They were interrupted by the RCMP constable who was leading a woman through the door. She was in her early forties with thick fair hair parted on one side and held away from her face with a clip. She was dressed in a flowered cotton dress, an old blue blazer, and sandals. She wore no make-up, and her eyes were raw.

'This is Mrs Hyde,' the constable said.

Croll stepped forward. 'Thanks for coming over. Did they tell you what we want?'

She nodded and pushed her hands into her jacket pockets.

'You were a friend of Mr Elton's, Miss Hyde? Did you know the house pretty well?'

'It's *Mrs* Hyde. My first husband died, too. I was Clive's fiancée.' She spoke carefully as if unsure how the words would come out.

She hasn't said much since she heard, Salter thought.

Croll continued. 'We'd like you to look around and tell us if anything is missing. Anything you can remember. Take a look now, and maybe later if you think of anything else you could come back or let us know.'

She looked around the room slowly, seeming more to avoid the objects she saw than search for anything missing. Then her gaze stopped at three shelves on the wall. 'There,' she said. 'All Clive's silver is gone.' She pointed. 'He had some silver mugs and things and a Victorian silver eggcup I gave him.' She stopped then, her voice breaking, put her hand back in her pocket and turned away from the two men. 'Sorry,' she said.

'That's all we need, Mrs Hyde. Thanks.' He called in the constable and told him to radio for a car to take her home.

She shook her head. 'I'm staying with a friend round the corner,' she said. 'I'll walk.'

The constable opened the door to let her out.

As the two men left the house, a dark blue battered pick-up truck pulled up by the front gate, and a weathered-looking middle-aged man wearing rubber boots and a curious-looking peaked cap with a high bonnet, somewhere between a baseball cap and a railroad engineer's, got out.

'Joe,' said Salter, surprised. 'What do you want?'

The man looked at Salter and at Croll and blinked. 'Sump'n wrong?' he asked.

'He asked you first,' Croll said. 'What are you doing here?'

Joe blinked again. 'I come to see Mr Elton,' he said. He looked past the two men to the Mountie guarding the door. 'I come to see if Mr Elton wanted a bit of fish. Is sump'n the matter with him?'

'He's dead, Joe,' Salter said. He turned to Croll. 'Joe operates a fishing-boat out of the harbour. We all buy our fish from him.'

'I know who Joe is,' Croll said. 'I live here.' He turned to the fisherman. 'You've lost a customer, Joe. Mr Elton was killed Saturday night. Don't you listen to the news?'

'Holy Jesus. Somebody *kilt* him? On Saturday?'

'That's right. I thought the whole Island knew by now.'

'Holy *Jeesus*.' Joe continued to stare at each man in turn. 'I never heard nothin' about it. I was away to a wedd'n on Saturday on the mainland. I just got back last night. I was calling in before I went down to the boat.'

'You start work late,' Croll said.

'We wasn't goin' out this morning. Just this afternoon with the tourists. Besides, I was still feeling a bit under the weather, like, from the wedd'n.' He looked up at the cottage again and shook his head. 'Holy Jesus,' he said again.

They left him there to recover, and drove to a coffee-shop in the main street.

Over a sandwich and a beer Croll became inquisitive about Salter's connection with the Island. Salter explained how he had met Annie while he was on vacation nearly twenty years before when Annie was the hostess at a resort hotel her father owned along the coast from Cavendish.

'Montagu owned that, too, did he? He's a big man in these parts, isn't he? How come you don't work for him?'

'Would you? Work for your father-in-law?'

'My father-in-law was a timekeeper for the mine in Sudbury. He didn't have any employees. But, no, probably not. What's your background, Salter? Where are you from? I know you're from away, as they say around here.'

'Toronto is where I'm from. I don't have any background.'

'Which part? I grew up in Toronto. In Swansea, actually, along the lakeshore.'

'Cabbagetown,' Salter said, then added, 'the old Cabbagetown, before it got fashionable. My old man repaired streetcars.'

'How did old Montagu take to his daughter marrying a cop from Cabbagetown?'

This was one question more than Croll was entitled to so early in their acquaintanceship, but Salter thought he knew where it came from. The relationship between the Mounties and the government, any government, was supposed to be conducted at arm's length. On the other hand, the Mounties, like any police force, knew who was in power. It was only human. And Salter's father-in-law was one of the powerful on the Island. So it was only human for Croll to wonder how far Salter was a Toronto cop on holiday, nobody of importance, or Montagu's son-in-law, whom he might be expected to treat with respect. And having wondered, it was also natural for Croll to be irritated that he was even wondering, and to be slightly rude, slightly patronizing of Salter to show he couldn't care less, one way or the other. All this Salter realized, but it didn't stop him wanting to push Croll back into his own territory.

'I have no idea,' Salter said. 'He might have been more pleased if I were in your mob. Then I could have worn a pointed hat at the wedding, like Smoky the Bear. But we're on good terms now. All I cared about was what his daughter thought, which is all I care about now.' He smiled to show he was just being cheeky, as Croll had been over-familiar. Then he added, 'I'll take you over to Montagu's and leave you there. You can send for a car when you're through. You don't need me around.'

Croll considered the offer. 'You in Homicide?' he asked.

'No, but my last three cases have involved homicide.' Salter explained how this had happened.

'Nor am I. We don't have a Homicide unit, as such, because we don't have homicides. This is the first on the Island in three years. Why don't you stay around and watch? You might be useful. I forgot, though. You're on holiday.'

'That's okay. I've got nothing better to do this afternoon. Sure, I'd like to. My father-in-law would fill me in afterwards, but I'd like to get a look at this Toronto dealer myself.'

So it was settled. Territories had been defined, roles exchanged, and the two men relaxed.

'How much is this thing worth?' Croll asked.

'Twenty thousand.'

'Who was going to ante up? The taxpayers?'

'No. My father-in-law and two other guys.'

'What was in it for them?'

'They just feel patriotic. They call themselves Friends of the Island.'

Croll adopted an expression of comic scepticism. 'That right? I know what Montagu's interest is. I just wondered about the other two.'

Salter accepted the provocation. 'So what is Montagu's interest?'

'Oh, he gets to be senator, didn't you know? He's been in line for some time. Party stalwart, chief bagman—he's got all the right credentials for the Senate. All he was waiting for was a vacancy and a change of government in Ottawa. Didn't he tell you?' Croll sat back, amused.

Salter allowed the Mountie his prescience, realizing that however it was qualified, he was probably right. 'Montagu will make as good a senator as most of them,' he said.

'Oh, sure. Better, probably.' Croll looked at his watch. 'We've got an hour yet. Got any ideas?'

Salter looked through the window of the café. The Island

was having a golden summer; only a few traces of cloud moved benevolently across the wide blue sky.

'We could walk around the harbour. I like doing that.'

'Let's go for a walk, then. I'll pay this. You can get it next time.

In the harbour, four or five boats were preparing to load up with tourists for an afternoon's mackerel fishing. All the boats were similar—wooden motor-driven launches about forty feet long with a tiny wheelhouse in front of the decked-over hold. They were adapted for tourist excursions by ranging ordinary wooden benches around the edge of the deck, placed so that the tourists could sit on a bench and fish over the side.

As they watched the fishermen putting the benches in place, the two policemen talked about Fehely, and his pursuit of the robber.

'He's keen,' Croll said with a grin. 'A real bird-dog. So he should be at his age. He spends most of his spare time thinking about this robber. He's got a theory that someone at the airport is keeping tabs on who leaves the Island for more than a day, and is feeding the information to the thief.'

'He told me.'

'So he's been keeping tabs himself. The trouble is that most weekends, when these things have been happening, there's usually more than one householder going to Montreal or Toronto for a few days. That's why they have a plane service. So Fehely has to choose the most likely house. So far he hasn't been lucky. While he watches one place, someone is breaking into another, twenty miles away. His theory may be all right, but he may never be able to prove it.' Croll smiled.

'He won't get a chance now, will he?'

'Not if Elton's killer and the regular thief are the same guy, and that seems likely, doesn't it?'

There was a shout from along the quay where a figure in

rubber boots and a strange-looking cap was putting some steps in place so that the tourists could board. 'You comin' wit' us, Mr Salter?' the man shouted.

'Not today, Joe. Mackerel don't bite when the wind is in the East.'

Joe nodded. 'Is that right? Maybe we'll catch a few before they realize which way the wind is blowing.' He kicked the steps into place and walked along the quay towards them.

'You ever go out with them?' Croll asked Salter.

'I've taken the kids out a couple of times. Mackerel are too easy, though.'

'Try the tuna-fishing.'

'I don't want to catch anything I can't lift.'

Now Joe was up with them, wiping his hands on his trousers. 'That's a terrible business with Mr Elton,' he said. 'He was a helluva nice fella. Wouldn't kick a stray cat, he wouldn't. Do you think you'll catch the bastard?'

'We'll catch him, don't worry,' Croll said.

'The same fella who's being doin' the robberies, d'ye think?'

Croll ignored the question. 'How well did you know him? Did he have any enemies?'

'Not a one. Not a damn one. I'm tellin' you he was a helluva decent fella. What about his ladyfriend? This'll be hard on her.'

'Do you know her?'

'A little bit. She's been teaching school here a long time. Mr Elton told me he was marryin' her. I was a bit surprised he hadn't tried it before at his age, but good luck to him. Now this. He wouldn't hurt a fly.'

'You got any ideas of your own who was doing the robberies, Joe?' Croll asked. He looked around the harbour. 'Anyone here have any ideas about that?'

Joe looked at Salter, then at Croll, then back to Salter. 'If I hear of anything like that, I'll let Mr Salter know. Bastard.' He adjusted his hat fractionally. No one had ever seen him without the hat and the Salters had speculated about why he never took it off and why it had such a high crown. Annie suspected he was totally bald and shy about it. Sheila tried her hand at interpretation, but got nowhere. Angus developed a tentative fantasy about a small creature that lived under the hat, but it was too derivative, of Jiminy Cricket, mostly. Salter's suggestion was that he kept an emergency supply of candy there, because Joe's other peculiarity was that he was constantly munching hard candy, chiefly fruitdrops, which made his breath thick and sweet.

Croll looked at his watch. 'Come on. We've killed enough time. Let's go and meet this dealer.'

CHAPTER 5

Barry Callendar looked like a caricature of a fatherly priest, or even a popular bishop. He filled his clothes tightly but not softly, without any overlapping fat. A tanned face was surmounted by a flat polished top edged with a fringe of groomed silver hair. His eyes twinkled through small round spectacles, and two rows of square white teeth smiled continually. He was wearing a grey lightweight suit and carrying a pearly-white raincoat that was the most expensive-looking garment Salter had ever seen that wasn't made of fur.

Montagu introduced him to the two policemen and Callendar made a cheerful remark about the sad circumstances of their meeting. When the four men were seated, Croll came to the point at once.

'We've been told that Mr Elton was in possession of this seal when he was killed. Is that right?'

'He certainly got it from me on Friday, and as far as I know brought it back with him. Haven't you found it yet?'

Callendar sought intimacy in his conversational style, closing in on his listener in earnest communion, nodding or shaking his head as he watched for agreement.

Croll said, 'Not unless we didn't recognize it. Can you describe it? What are we looking for? How big is it? How heavy?'

'About the size of a small ashtray,' Callendar said after a pause during which he searched Croll's face. 'A thin one. I'd say it weighed about half a pound.'

'How was it wrapped?'

'I beg your pardon?' Callendar continued to smile at Croll, but the wattage was reduced slightly. Salter, watching him, wondered whether he smiled at funerals. The features seemed to be set in a permanent spasm of joy.

'How do you mean—"wrapped"?' Callendar asked.

'I mean what did you give him to carry it in? He didn't fly back from Toronto waving it about, did he?'

Callendar pushed up his rheostat and a chuckle came out. 'I see what you mean. No, I put it in a plain brown bag.'

'How did it come from the original owner? Did he bring it to you, by the way?'

'Yes, yes, he brought it himself.'

'Well, did *he* wrap it up? And did you take his wrapping off? I want to know what we are looking for.'

'Of course. No, he had it sewn in canvas, which we cut off to look at it.'

'And did you sew it back up before you put it in the plain brown bag?'

'You know, I'm not sure. Wait a minute.' He made a dumbshow of remembering, moving his hands to imitate handling an object, smoothing the creases out and finally putting it in a bag. 'No,' he said triumphantly, 'We just rewrapped it in the canvas and put it in the bag.'

'So we are looking for a canvas-covered thing about the size of a small ashtray. Was the canvas clean or dirty?'

'Oh, *clean*.' He turned to Salter suddenly, 'New, I would think.'

'All right. Now who else knew he had the seal?'

'No one in Toronto. I don't have an assistant. No one, except me.'

'When he left you, do you know where he went?'

'Straight to the airport, I'm sure. He had his overnight bag with him, and I called for a cab.'

'You said on Friday? He came back on Saturday.'

'Saturday, I mean.' He nodded several times.

'Did he put the seal in the bag?'

Again Callendar made a show of remembering. 'Yes. Yes, he did.'

'Why was he picking it up? He hadn't paid you for it, had he?'

'I had no fears on that score. I still don't. I'm sure you people—' here he looked at Montagu—'will honour your obligations. The seal *was* delivered and now the money is owing.'

'We have only your word for the fact that it was delivered. Everyone here was under the impression that it would be delivered next week. Elton was supposed to go and get it.'

'I know. That's why I'm here to tell you otherwise. And to urge you to find it.' Callendar sat back and smiled all round.

'If we don't find it, we'll have to find some other way of establishing that the seal was handed over. You could prove from your principal that you had it, of course.'

'No, I couldn't. My principal demands total anonymity. He will refuse to come forward, and I have agreed to that from the beginning. No, if the seal doesn't turn up, and I can't prove that I handed it over, as I *can't*, I may have to make the loss good myself, unless you people will accept responsibility.' He looked at Montagu.

'Let's talk about that when the time comes,' Montagu

interrupted. 'In the meantime, let's find the seal, eh, Brian?'

Croll had not taken his eyes off the dealer. 'Which cab company in Toronto did you call, Mr Callendar? We can check at that end. Maybe the driver will remember him and what he was carrying.'

'I'll try and remember. I just flipped through the Yellow Pages.'

'It's a twenty-dollar fare, and it would have gone through the despatcher. There'll be a record,' Salter said.

Callendar turned to Salter, looking at him expectantly.

Croll rose to his feet. 'That's it, then. I'll take you back, Salter. Are you staying on the Island, sir?' he asked Callendar.

'For a night, anyway,' Callendar said. 'I can't stay much longer. I'm booked into the Marlin Motel in Marlow, and here's my Toronto number.' He handed over a card. 'Dear, dear, dear. We seem to be forgetting poor Clive. Find the seal, by all means, but find the swine who killed Clive. That's the important thing, isn't it?' He smiled a brilliant sad smile.

Croll paused with Callendar's card in his hand. 'How well did you get to know Elton?' he asked Callendar.

'Not at all, really. Oddly enough, I *had* met him once before when he came into my store and bought a little silver desk set that was probably made by someone around here. He reminded me of it on Friday, but I didn't really remember him.'

'A tray with grooves in it?'

'That's it. No, I got in touch with the government here, and Mr Montagu replied, and then I was told that a Mr Clive Elton would be in charge of negotiations. He came to Toronto about three weeks ago, and we settled on a price. The next time I saw him was on the weekend. An awfully nice man, and very knowledgeable,' he added, addressing Montagu.

'Did you ever visit him here?'

Callendar shook his head. 'This is my first visit to the Cradle of Confederation.'

'All right.' Croll nodded to Callendar. To Montagu, he said, 'I'll be in touch tomorrow. Let's go, Salter.'

'Hell of a story, isn't it?' Croll said in the car on their way back to Cavendish.

Salter laughed. 'Sounds a little phoney, doesn't it? But those guys all sound as though they're working a swindle, because they are always protecting their information. They're dealers, and they'd be out of business if the customers knew as much as they did. But you heard Montagu. He insured himself against any funny business with fakes and stuff. If this dealer is reputable, and I'll bet Montagu or Elton already made sure of that, then Montagu had nothing to worry about.'

'He does now, though, doesn't he?'

'Why?' Salter knew the answer, but the conversation allowed him to think along with Croll, and test his own responses.

'We only have Callendar's word for it that Elton brought the thing back with him. If Elton didn't tell anyone about it, his girlfriend, say, then we'll still only have his word. What I mean is, we *might* be able to confirm that Elton brought it back, but we'll never be able to prove that he didn't.'

'So?'

'Don't piss around, Salter. You know what I mean. It could be this dealer saw a chance for himself. When he heard that Elton went tits-up in a robbery, he had a nice little scam handed to him on a plate. Montagu and the other people here can confirm that all the other arrangements were in place, and Callendar comes up with this story and appeals for payment on the grounds that he's done his bit.' Croll pulled over to the side of the road and stopped the car. 'What do you think?'

Salter roared with laughter. 'What the hell do they teach you in that training college in Saskatchewan? On Saturday night a guy named Elton became one victim of a series of robberies. He disturbed the robber and got killed. By a coincidence he happened to have something valuable in the house. That's it. What are you looking for, for Christ's sake?'

But Croll wasn't to be laughed off. 'That guy Callendar,' he said. 'He looks totally phoney to me.'

'What's phoney about him is this idea that someone knew Elton had the seal and waylaid him. Now that you know the other stuff is missing, you can forget about it. As an idea, I mean. But I wouldn't forget that it's Callendar's idea.'

Croll thought this through. 'You don't think maybe Callendar still has the seal? Hoping to get paid and sell it again?'

'It never occurred to me.'

Croll shook his head, changing his mind. 'It's too risky. If the thing turned up in twenty years we'd still nail him.'

Salter shrugged. Whatever you say, he thought. I'm on holiday myself.

Croll brooded some more. 'It's possible,' he said. 'He may not have realized at the time that he'd never be able to sell it again—the idea of having it twice would be his first reaction. Okay. Let's file that one for a minute. He's probably just in a panic, running down here to protect his interests. If he can persuade your father-in-law that he handed the seal over, then Montagu will probably pay him.'

'If Montagu believes him, he'll pay him. He's an honourable man, as they say.'

'Aren't they all? That's probably it, then. Twenty thousand is worth flying down for. Let's take him at his word.' Croll had another thought. 'This anonymous principal? You think he exists?'

'Do you think Callendar made him up?'

'Could be. I think I'll check up on Callendar a little. Ask

your father-in-law how he sounded when he was told about Elton. Ask him if Callendar's response sounded genuine.'

'You should have a look at the original correspondence between Callendar and the government if you're going to go after Callendar, the mastermind.'

'Anything else I have to do?'

'I'm just thinking out loud.'

'I know. Very insulting it is, too.' Croll laughed. 'Don't mind me, Salter. I enjoy your company, but your connections make me nervous.

The next morning Salter drove Annie and Sheila into Charlottetown to catch the plane for a day's outing to Halifax and returned to Marlow to pick up Angus for a morning's golf.

They played nine holes before Angus got thirsty and they stopped for a soft drink at the clubhouse. Constable Fehely was standing in the door as they approached.

'I saw you putting out the ninth as I was driving by,' he said. 'How are you getting on, Angus?'

'Not bad, Mr Fehely. My dad is still beating me, though.'

'Can you join us for the last nine, Dennis?' After nine holes Salter and Angus had run out of chat.

The constable shook his head. 'We're short-staffed. I'll drink a pop with you, though.'

Salter bought a round of soft drinks and they walked out to a picnic table.

'I was just up to see Elton's girlfriend,' Fehely said.

'The man who was killed?' Angus asked.

'That's right.'

'But he was so *old*. It must have been platonic.'

'He was younger than me,' Salter said. Angus blushed. Fehely said, 'They were going to be married soon. She is still very cut up about it.'

'She looked bad when I saw her.'

'How old is she?' Angus asked.

'I'd say in her early forties.'

'About the same age as Eleanor,' Salter pointed out. 'Does *she* look so old?'

'No, that's right. She doesn't seem old at all.' Angus thought for a moment. 'How old is Mum?'

'Forty-one,' Salter said, and watched Angus's face as the boy reassembled his assumptions about the sex life of geriatrics.

'She was with Elton the night he got killed, wasn't she?' Salter asked.

'That's right.' Fehely glanced at Angus. 'He left her place about two o'clock and walked home.' He looked quickly at Angus again. 'Apparently they sort of got engaged that night, though they had been planning to for some time. He was going to take them to Europe for a honeymoon, and then they were coming back to live in his house. She has a little apartment over a hardware store.'

Salter picked over the conversations of the last two days. 'She collected him from the airport on Saturday, didn't she? Have you tried to fit him into your theory?'

'Only like this. Someone who knew him saw him leave. He was booked to come back on Sunday. A couple of people knew that, and he might have mentioned it to anyone at the airport. He could have come back without anyone noticing, especially since she picked him up.'

Salter nodded. 'And if anyone checked his house it would have been dark all evening. And on Friday night.'

'Right. So we're still hoping for a connection.'

'What about the seal?' Salter turned to Angus. 'Has anyone mentioned the seal around the house?'

'No. What seal?'

'I'll tell you later. In the meantime keep it to yourself even at home.

'Don't tell Sheila, you mean?'

'Don't tell *anyone*.'

'Okay, but *you* tell *me*.'

Salter promised and turned back to Fehely. 'Does she remember it?' He had a sudden thought. 'He didn't leave it with her, did he? Christ, he walked home, so . . .'

Fehely laughed and shook his head. 'My staff sergeant thought of that. No. She said when she met him he just had his travelling bag, and the seal must have been in that. She took him back to his house to change his clothes before dinner, and waited for him downstairs. When he was cleaned up they drove to her apartment.'

'Didn't he mention the seal? Didn't she know about it?'

'Not really. She knew he'd gone to Toronto to see a man for the government. She said he was mysterious and excited about the trip, but he wouldn't tell her what it was all about.'

'I wonder why? It was confidential all right, but you would have expected him to drop a hint to her.'

'This is a very small island. She was a bit proud of him, I reckon. She talked about him being on government work as though he was with the CIA. She seemed to think I wouldn't know anything about it. He must have made it sound very important and hush-hush.'

'So she never saw the thing.'

'No. They came back to the house, he went up and changed, and that was that.'

'And the bag?'

'That was tucked away in a cupboard, empty. He'd put his dirty laundry in the clothes basket in the bedroom.'

'And probably left the seal in the bedroom.'

'It wasn't there when we looked,' Fehely said.

'I know. What about the people who knew he was going to be away? Who were they?'

'One man, and a secretary. Nothing there. And the girl-friend, of course.'

'Did *she* think he was coming back on Sunday?'

'That's right. He called from Toronto on Saturday to say there was no reason to stay over. So they planned to have dinner together at her place, and she picked him up at the airport, like I said.'

'And she didn't know anything about why he was in Toronto?'

'On government business. She kept implying that I wasn't important enough to be in on Elton's secret mission, so I let her know I knew what it was, just to see if she really knew, but she didn't.'

'Was she his mistress?' Angus asked. He had been growing up rapidly as they talked.

'They were engaged.' Salter looked to Fehely for help.

'I'm sort of engaged myself,' Fehely said. 'But I wouldn't like Pat to catch me calling her my mistress. I don't think there are any mistresses on the Island. You have to be married to have a mistress, don't you, Mr Salter?'

'So they tell me. How's the rest of your theory coming?'

'I've got it mapped out. If you want to come by the detachment, I'll show you. We'd have to go now, though.'

'Do you mind, Angus?'

Angus shook his head politely. 'That's all right. I've had enough. But would you watch me try a couple of drives, Mr Fehely? I'm doing something funny with my swing.'

After a brief lesson from Fehely, Angus was happy to be driven home. Salter dropped him off and drove over to the Cavendish detachment where Fehely was waiting for him, a map of the Island spread out on his desk.

'Each one of these crosses marks a robbery of someone who was on the mainland at the time,' Fehely said. 'I've got the statements from the owners about the way they left the Island. Most of them took cabs to the airport, and some of them remember which cab company. A couple even remember the drivers.'

'What about the ones who didn't take cabs?'

'They left their cars at the airport. It's pretty easy for someone to spot which cars are being left overnight.'

'Then they'd have to find out who owns the car. They'd

need a contact in the Licence Bureau. It's getting pretty complicated, Dennis.'

'Yeah, I know. It has to be something like this, though. It's too much of a coincidence. A guy leaves the Island and his house is robbed, so someone must know he is leaving.'

'The whole family would have to be away, wouldn't they? The house is always empty.'

Fehely nodded. He pushed the map to one side, discouraged.

'They made a mistake with Elton, didn't they? He came back too early,' Salter said.

'Right. He went out on a Friday and was booked back on Sunday. So whoever killed him must have thought he'd be away that night. Doesn't that prove my point?'

'How did he get out to the airport?'

'I don't know yet. He was working in his office on Friday morning. He probably caught a ride with someone.'

'If he did, it kind of shoots your theory all to hell, doesn't it? Unless he was seen by someone who knew him, one of these cabbies, getting on the plane with an overnight bag. Even then they wouldn't know how long he was going to be away for. I wish you luck, Dennis, but it doesn't look too promising. Got any other leads?'

'I've made a list of all the stuff that could be traced. None of it has turned up around here, or in Halifax or Moncton. I'm asking the Fraud squads in Montreal and Toronto to see if there's any sign of it there.'

'What kind of stuff?'

'Wedding rings, watches—all small stuff. This guy wouldn't take anything big or very valuable that would be hard to get rid of—just money and small jewellery. Even so, he had to get rid of it off the Island.'

'So we are talking about a petty crook. An accidental killer, if it's the same guy. Have you tried the other end? Looked for someone who makes regular trips to Toronto?' Salter looked at the map. 'Yeah, Toronto.'

'Why? Why not Montreal?'

'The odds are better for one thing. What's the French population of the Island? Fifteen per cent? And most of them live up the other end. So it's better than six to one that the guy you're looking for is English-speaking, which means Toronto, where all the English-speaking maritimers go when there's no work around here. Another thing, if your theory has anything in it, whoever was robbing the houses knows who the owners are, and since they are all Anglos, he probably is, too. So who can you find who travels to Toronto regularly, or often, anyway? Put the word out to Toronto for an Islander who is going around town with stuff to sell. I doubt if this guy's got very good connections, so someone might have come across him toting a bag full of rings around the beer parlours. Tell someone to ask our people. Tell them to try that pub on Spadina Avenue where all the maritimers hang out.'

'You serious?'

Salter considered. 'Yeah, I think I am. Is your boss in, now? Maybe I'll say hello.'

'He's busy right now. He's just talking to one of the local lads about where he was on Saturday night.'

Standard procedure. Salter watched as a second constable came in from the outside with another man in tow. 'Give the officer your name,' the Mountie said, 'then sit down and keep your mouth shut.'

'Tell your staff sergeant I was in,' Salter said. 'I'll give him a call later.'

He had been hoping to tag along with the investigation for an hour or two, but now he was at a slight loss for something to do. A pleasant image floated into his mind; he decided it was his social duty to call on Eleanor Vail to find out if she had everything she needed.

A familiar-looking pick-up truck parked outside the door took some of the pleasure away from his call. He knocked, and Eleanor opened the door and hauled him inside with an enthusiastic welcome, pushing him into the kitchen where he found another visitor, drinking coffee. A man in his early forties, tall, thin, with dark curly hair and a cared-for moustache. His one-or-two-day-old beard gave no impression of neglect, but rather of someone resting his face between engagements, the Sunday-morning beard of a weekend sailor. Diamond Jim Brady, the dealer and carpenter.

'Jim's making me a table,' Eleanor said. 'Sit down, Charlie. Thanks for putting me on to Jim. He's been wonderful. He's put new locks on all the doors, fixed the gate, and now he's making me a table to type on. The cottage is lovely but I don't have anywhere to type. I need to spread myself, so Jim is going to find me a door and put it on legs, aren't you, Jim? And he's going to bring me some moonshine.' She giggled. 'Now, coffee?'

Salter accepted a cup and sat down. 'You making it or just selling it?' he asked Brady.

'I know where I can get some. Why? You want some?'

'No, I just wanted to know so I could tell the Mounties.'

'That's right. I've seen you riding around with those guys.' Brady grinned over his coffee mug. 'They already know where to get it.'

'How much?'

'Like, how much a gallon?'

Salter nodded.

'Fifty dollars. That's what I hear.'

Salter appeared to consider. 'You'll get caught,' he said finally. 'But I could use your help on something else. My wife bought an old chopping block at an auction the other day, but no one can lift the thing. You know someone who could give you a hand to deliver it to our place?'

'How big is it?'

'About three feet by four feet, she says.'

'A real block?'

'It's two feet thick.'

'I looked the stuff over at that auction. The old Winter place? Toronto guy? Moved to England?'

'I don't know.'

'Friday, wasn't it?'

'That's right.'

'That's the only one, then. I never saw a block. How much did she give for it?'

'Two dollars,' Salter lied.

'Tell her I'll give her fifty,' Brady said. 'I have a customer looking for one of them.'

'No dice. She's been looking for one like this for years. Will you move it?'

'I'll have to get some help. Take about three hours all told, for the two of us.'

'How much?'

'Say forty-five?'

'Screw you. I'll get Joe 'n' Eddie. They've got a truck.'

Brady laughed. 'If she's in no hurry I'll bring it over when I'm passing. I'll charge you for the helper, for loading it. I'll throw my labour in for all the business you're bringing me.' He nodded in Eleanor's direction. 'You can help me unload it.'

They finished their coffee and Brady stood up. He turned to Eleanor. 'If you're going to be home this afternoon, I'll bring that table by. I'll set it up in the morning.'

'Lovely. I'll be here,' Eleanor said. 'Don't go, Charlie. We'll have some more coffee.' She accompanied Brady to the door for a final word. When she returned she had the rosy look of a woman who has shared her kitchen with two men she liked. 'More coffee?' she asked again.

He pushed his cup forward, telling himself that the coffee here was very good. 'Diamond Jim fixing you up, is he?'

'Oh, he's been wonderful. I've found lots for him to do. He's going to look for a rocking-chair for me so I can sit and rock on the porch in the afternoons. He's lovely. And your chicken man called. I see why Angus calls him the lava man. Now all I need is to find some free-range lobsters.'

'Tom Gush will sell you some. He's a lobster fisherman, too. Have you been down to the harbour yet? For fish?'

'No, I'm waiting for Angus to take me.'

'I'll take you down if you like. They should be coming in about now.'

Eleanor looked slightly confused. 'No, Angus will be disappointed. But if you are going, perhaps you could bring me something back. A little cod, enough for two?'

Salter had not planned to go, but he changed his mind on the spot. 'I'll drop it off before lunch.' He stood up.

'Any time later would be fine. Don't go out of your way.'

'No sweat. Anything else you need?'

'No, but I want to have you and Annie to dinner next Tuesday or Wednesday. And Sheila, of course. Which is the best day for you?'

'I'll ask Annie. Are you getting any work done?'

'Not really. I'm enjoying myself too much playing house. I will, though. As soon as the rocking-chair arrives.'

Salter drove down to the harbour and parked his car where he could see the wharf. Joe 'n' Eddie had brought in the day's catch and were working to unload it and clean up the boat for the afternoon's tourists. Seated on a bench watching them was Barry Callendar, looking completely incongruous among the ropes and lobster pots, like someone who has wandered on to the scene of a movie set in another age. 'Hey,' Salter said, sitting down beside him. 'I thought you would have gone back by now.'

'Ah, there, Inspector. I had some second thoughts. It occurred to me that this is a very small island and Sergeant Croll would probably find the killer very quickly, in which case the seal would turn up and I would be able to get my money right away.'

'I think you'll get your money. And you're probably right, Croll will flush him out before too long. What are you going to do around here?' He waved towards the dock.

'Be a tourist for a few hours. And you?'

'I came by to get some fish from Joe 'n' Eddie there.'

Callendar looked where he was pointing. 'They are the local harvesters of the sea, are they?' He smiled his brilliant smile.

'Some of them. The ones we all know. But half a dozen boats use this harbour.'

'Fishing-boats?'

'Two or three of them double as tourist boats during the season. Like these guys.'

'Does one have to book?'

'You want to go?' He looked at Callendar's beautiful grey suit, his Italian-looking shoes, and the white raincoat.

Callendar followed Salter's glance. 'Not dressed for it, I suppose.'

'It can get a bit messy. If you really want to go I can find you a slicker and a pair of boots.' It was a gesture only, and he was surprised when Callendar took him seriously.

'Could you? I don't know anything about fishing, though.'

'You don't have to. This isn't really fishing. They give you a piece of string with a hook on it, and you put a bit of fish on the hook—I'll do that for you, if you want—and throw it over the side.' Why am I doing this? Salter wondered. Because I might as well do this as anything else.

'You know, I *would* like to try,' Callendar said shyly.

'Let's go and see Joe.'

Along the quay the unloading was finished, and Eddie was washing the deck of the boat with a hose. They found Joe inside the shed, weighing the catch before handing it over to the wholesaler. Salter lifted a small cod off the pile of fish on the floor of the warehouse. 'How much for this one, Joe?'

'A dollar. Gimme the money later.' He spread his hands to show he was covered in fish scales, and went back to shovelling fish.

They watched him finish, and when he had sluiced his

hands under a tap, Salter produced a dollar bill.

'Hang on,' Joe said. 'I'll git you a bag.' He produced a plastic bag from a nest of rubbish in the corner of the shed, slid the fish in and handed it to Salter.

'You going out this afternoon?' Salter asked. 'Mr Callendar wants to go fishing. I'll come out with him.'

'Oh, ah. I'll save you a couple of seats. On your holidays, are you?' he asked Callendar.

'Mr Callendar's a friend of Clive Elton,' Salter said. 'He came down to see if there was anything he could do.'

'Pal of his, were you?'

'A business associate, really.' Callendar smiled. 'He was one of my clients. I'm in the antique business, and Mr Elton and I were negotiating for something he wanted.'

'You from Toronto?' Joe asked.

'Yes.'

Joe considered him for a few moments. 'Bad business,' he said.

'Did you know Clive?'

'Mr Elton? Oh, ah. You know pretty well everyone about here, one way or the other.'

'Was he a "pal"?' Callendar asked putting the colloquialism in quotation marks.

'He was a client o' mine,' Joe said. 'He bought the odd bit of fish from me.'

The three men stood there without any more to say, and Joe wiped his hands on his trousers. 'I'll see yez this afternoon, then,' he said. He turned away to wash his boots off under the tap.

Callendar walked back with Salter to his car, where Salter offered the dealer a ride back to his motel. Callendar refused. 'I think I'll just poodle about here for a while. Find a place for a beer and a sandwich. What time should we meet?'

'They go out about two o'clock. I'll meet you here about a quarter to.'

'Jolly good. Let's hope they're biting, eh?'

Salter drove off, leaving Callendar surveying the scene, choosing a route for a stroll. When he called at Eleanor's door a few minutes late, fish in hand, he was greeted with the usual 'lovely', and he followed Eleanor into the kitchen where he found Brady again, drinking soup.

'Come and sit down, Charlie. Have some soup,' Eleanor said.

Salter sat down, feeling like a second-comer, slightly foolish, and irritated. 'Annie and Sheila are in Halifax,' he said, wondering if he had already said that once that day.

'Then it's my job to feed you,' Eleanor said. 'Jim brought me some lovely ham. He knows a man who cures his own.'

'Around here?'

'Up by St Louis. You want me to get you some?'

'I'll ask my wife.' There was a long pause as he and Brady waited for the other to speak. Eleanor produced bread and butter and the three of them constructed sandwiches.

'What are you going to do with yourself, this afternoon?' Eleanor asked Salter when they were settled in, munching.

'I'm going out on one of the fishing-boats, catch some mackerel.'

'With the tourists?' Brady asked. There was some amusement in his voice, a small intonation, that suggested there were other ways for a grown-up Islander to spend his time, more serious ways of fishing. 'Taking the kids?' he added, offering Salter an out.

'They've gone sailing,' Salter said. Then, to justify himself, 'I met the Toronto dealer on the dock, and he wanted to try it so I said I'd go out with him.'

'Who's that, then?' Brady asked.

'He's someone who knew Clive Elton, the guy who was killed on Saturday. He came down to see if he could identify anything that was stolen. Elton bought things from him in Toronto.'

'He's staying around for a bit, is he?'

'For a day or so, anyway, in case they catch the guy right

away. If he's caught with anything on him, then this dealer might recognize it.'

'Personally, I feel quite safe now,' Eleanor said. 'Jim's putting locks on everything.'

'I don't think you'll have to worry. If it's the same guy, he won't be robbing anyone for a while, if ever. He'll stay right out of sight,' Brady said judiciously. 'Did he get away with much? The guy who killed Elton?'

Salter considered the question. 'I guess they don't know. That's why the dealer is here.'

Brady belched lightly and stood up. 'I've got that door on the truck. I'll bring it in and go get the legs.'

Salter remained seated over his coffee as Brady went out. What he would like to do, he decided, was drink coffee for an hour with Eleanor without Brady around.

Brady reappeared with the door and propped it against the wall. 'I was thinking,' he said. 'Those metal legs from the lumber company cost a bit. I could put it together a lot cheaper with some four-by-fours. Do you mind if it looks a bit clumsy?'

Eleanor shook her head. 'As long as it's solid. I can't have a wobbly surface when I'm trying to bear down.'

'I think four-by-fours would be a' lot more solid.'

Screw this, thought Salter. He stood up. 'I've got to go,' he said. 'By the way, we are going to one of those lobster suppers we told you about tonight. Are you interested?'

'Mmmm. Love to. What time?'

'We'll pick you up at six.'

'Right you are, Charlie. Thanks for the lovely fish. Oh, but . . . never mind, I'll eat it tomorrow. See you at six, then.' She turned back to Brady. 'Do you want a tape-measure to get the height?'

Salter left them engrossed in their problem.

CHAPTER 6

He drove home to pick up the boots and slicker and returned to the harbour where he found Callendar waiting, watching the tourists choose which boat they would go fishing in. Salter produced the boots and raincoat, and Callendar took off his shoes and dressed up. 'Yo ho ho and a bottle of rum,' he said, standing up and kicking his feet in a little jig. 'Do I really need the coat? You haven't got one.' In the ankle-length black slicker, Callendar now looked like the monk who loved venery.

'I can change when I'm through. You can't. And some time this afternoon you are going to get fish blood on you.'

Callendar fastened the slicker at his throat and pronounced himself ready. Salter locked Callendar's clothes in his car and they walked over to the boat where Joe found them two seats at the back and handed them their lines.

'Give me a cod line, Joe,' Salter said. Joe took back the spool of thin line and exchanged it for a much thicker line wound around a wooden frame.

'Why haven't I got one of those?' Callendar asked.

'You want to catch some fish,' Salter said. 'I've done my share of mackerel fishing, so I'm going to jig for cod. I might catch one all afternoon. You watch me.'

Four or five tourists were now aboard. Joe cast off and Eddie started the engine, and they headed for the mouth of the harbour. They chugged out to sea for about twenty minutes, then Joe and Eddie exchanged shouts at what looked like a small rainstorm about fifty feet across that passed by the boat, making the surface dance.

'Mackerel,' Salter said.

Eddie stopped the engine and let the anchor go. The tourists waited. From a storage box in the middle of the

boat, Joe took out a fish and cut it into small strips, then
went round the boat distributing the bait to the waiting
passengers. They baited their hooks under Joe's direction
and threw the lines out, and almost immediately began
hauling in mackerel while Joe and Eddie circled the boat,
unhooking fish, baiting hooks and adjusting the lines of the
one or two who did not catch fish immediately. Salter put
a lump of fish on his heavily weighted line, dropped it
overboard and began the slow regular jigging that was
meant to attract a cod. Callendar caught his first mackerel
within a few minutes which excited him enormously, and
he settle down to enjoy himself, handing his line to Salter
whenever he caught a fish to unhook the catch and rebait
the hook.

They fished for two hours and had pretty good luck. Every
ten minutes or so a school of mackerel would race past the
boat, shaking the surface of the water from below, making
the sea sparkle as they passed. When this happened, everyone caught two or three fish in quick succession. Then they
waited for the next school. As always, one man caught
nothing. With a line that was baited identically with everyone else's, and fishing at exactly the same depth, he failed
to get a single bite while on either side his wife and son
hauled them in with every cast. Joe tried everything for the
man, holding the line himself (when the fish immediately
started biting), moving him to different places on the boat,
cutting him extra-succulent pieces of bait. Nothing worked.
At one point the man insisted on changing places with his
ten-year-old son, but that didn't work either. After an hour
he quarrelled with his wife and told the kid to stop shouting
'Another one!' every goddamn time he caught a fish. He
spent the last half-hour sulking and looking at his watch.

Salter jigged away steadily and talked to Callendar in a
general way about the antique business. The matter of the
seal being confidential, they avoided talking about it openly,
but they managed to touch on Elton's death in general,

guarded terms. They settled on an elementary code for discussing the case, so that Elton's name would not have to be mentioned. Elton was 'my client' and the killer became 'our friend'. The authorities—the cabinet, the RCMP, Salter's father-in-law—became 'you people'.

'I doubt that our friend knows what he's got,' Callendar said at one point. 'I'm afraid he'll just dump it somewhere.'

'If he does, someone will pick it up. You'll be all right.'

Joe came over to see how Salter was getting on, and urged him for the good of the boat to go after mackerel, but Salter persisted with his hunt for cod.

'If he doesn't, and you don't catch the fellow, what will you do?' Callendar asked.

Salter waited until Joe had moved away. 'Croll?' he asked. 'I don't know. He isn't too concerned about your problem. He just wants to get his hands on our friend. But he might think it would be a good idea to publicize the loss of this thing. That might help you.'

'Why? Surely that would take away a lot of the reason you people are doing this. I mean the surprise and all that.'

'Finding our friend takes priority. Croll may decide to advertise—tell the story—because someone might have seen it who will recognize it. If Croll put up a reward for it, it would set such a person to thinking hard as to where he had seen it lately. Our friend might have got it in the first trip and gone back for more, then got disturbed by your client. It might still be in the truck or car he used, and it might have been seen by someone else who'll know from the advertisement what he's seen. Croll will try everything. It's like jigging for cod.'

'Of course. But if he finds our friend first he won't have to advertise, will he?'

Salter got a bite. With a little effort, suitable for a four- or five-pound cod, he hauled his line to the surface while everyone watched. He lifted out a small, revolting-looking fish, orange-coloured with a bubble of stomach protruding from its mouth, which even Joe was reluctant to handle, dealing with it by beating it against the side of the boat until the fish dropped off.

'What the hell was that?' Salter asked.

'Blowfish,' Joe said, which Salter guessed was his term for anything uneatable.

The conversation turned back to fishing. Salter continued to hope for a cod, while Callendar sat and watched, his tiny enthusiasm for fishing having been punctured by the sight of what he might catch.

Some of the other tourists were becoming slightly bored, too, and Joe made a business about being concerned with an approaching storm, pulled up the anchor and turned for home. When they docked, Callendar changed back into his shoes and Salter gave him a ride back to his motel. From there he drove to the airport where he was to meet Annie and Sheila.

Although he had very little faith in Dennis Fehely's theory, he had some time to kill so he strolled around the airport, noting the way the cabs worked. It was barely possible that someone—a cab-driver or group of drivers, the security guards, the check-out clerk, even the coffee-shop waitress —would be able to keep an eye on the comings and goings of the travellers, but small as the Island was, it seemed unlikely that anyone would know everybody. If a prominent Island family took a trip together, someone might take note, but Elton was a single, not-very-well-known bachelor; it was unlikely that anyone would have noticed him. In any case, Salter reminded himself, Elton did not take a cab to the airport. But he did come back a day early, changing his reservation from Sunday to Saturday.

The plane from Halifax arrived, Salter collected his womenfolk and drove them home.

'What did you do today, Charlie?' Annie asked. Her voice was bright and artificial. That plus his elementary knowledge of body language—the two women were sitting as far away from each other as possible in opposite corners of the back seat—suggested to Salter that Annie just wanted to hear someone else's voice for a while, someone other than Sheila.

'I went fishing,' he said, trying to make it sound interesting.

'On your own?'

'No, I took that dealer from Toronto.'

'Catch anything to eat?'

'No. Oh, I found someone to move your block. Jim Brady will do it.'

'Oh, good. Where did you run into him?'

'At Eleanor Vail's. I called in to see if she wanted to go down to the harbour to buy some fish. Brady was there fixing her a table. He knows someone who smokes his own hams.'

'Huh?'

'Ham. We had some for lunch which he'd brought.'

'You and Brady had lunch with Eleanor?'

'Yeah. She couldn't come down to the harbour so I brought her a small cod, and when I took it back she and Brady were eating lunch, so I joined them. She wants us to go over for dinner one night next week. I told her you'd let her know which.'

'Sounds like she's keeping open house,' Sheila said. 'Who else was she feeding today?'

There was a pause while Salter looked at her in his rear-view mirror. 'I didn't see anyone else,' he said. 'Brady is fixing up her table, and I brought her some fish, as promised. But I was only there for an hour. After me, I expect the septic tank man and the local well-digger called in. She probably had breakfast with the mailman.'

'Don't get defensive, Charlie. I was only joking.'

Annie said, 'Can we change the topic? Want to know what I bought in Halifax?'

The lobster supper took place in the church hall of a nearby village. The food was good, though a shade plentiful for Toronto appetites: lobster, bread, salad, potatoes, strawberry shortcake and coffee. All served by the ladies of the church.

'Do you have any chow-chow?' Eleanor asked.

'What the heck's that?' Angus said.

'Jim told me about it. It's a pickle they make on the Island.'

'We don't serve it with lobster,' the waitress said. 'Some places, maybe, not here. Chow-chow you eat with cod.'

'I must get some,' Eleanor said. Then, 'I see what Jim meant.'

The others waited to hear what Brady had said.

'I was asking him about why there are so few restaurants. He said it was hard to make a living with a year-round restaurant, and the season was too short to make it just in the summer. These lobster suppers look after the tourists, and there's no overhead and no staff to lay off in the winter. Hard to compete with.'

'Is Brady thinking of opening a restaurant?' Salter asked.

'Oh no. He probably could, though. That man seems able to do anything.'

'I guess that's why he's on the Island, doing odd jobs.'

He smiled when he said it, but Eleanor blinked and Salter tried to soften it. 'He's probably right about the restaurants. I never thought of it.'

But he didn't fool Annie, and later, in bed, she pointed out to him that if Eleanor Vail found Brady intriguing that was nice for her and no business of his.

The next morning Angus decided he wanted to go sailing again. 'We could play golf this afternoon,' he offered. 'I could take one of the cars and be back for lunch.'

'We're going shopping,' Annie said. 'We'll take you in and bring you back at noon.'

'I'll pick him up,' Salter said. 'I want to talk to your father at some point today.'

'Then why not come with us?'

'No, that's all right. You go ahead. I have a couple of things I want to do around here first.'

'Like what?' Annie looked at him, and seeing a man who did not want to be questioned, said no more.

When they had gone, Salter jumped into the car and drove over to Cavendish to see how the case was going.

Fehely met him in the outer room as if he had been waiting for him. 'We've put out the word in Toronto,' he said. 'And I've been checking down at the ferries like you suggested. We've had a man at the Borden ferry ever since Elton was killed. He's checking with the staff to make a list of anyone who makes the trip on a regular basis.'

'Good luck,' Salter said automatically. It had been no more than a casual suggestion, and he expected nothing to come of it. It was slightly embarrassing to be taken so seriously. At the same time, he was struck with the advantages of policing an island that could be sealed off when a major crime was committed. 'Is your boss in?' he asked.

Fehely nodded. 'He's on his own. You can go right in.'

'I was on my way to see my father-in-law,' Salter said, after Croll had gestured him to a chair. 'But I spent yesterday afternoon with that dealer, Callendar. I thought you might like to know what they're thinking.'

'They?'

'Well, Callendar. But I think Montagu will agree.'

'Where did you meet up with Callendar?'

'I took him out fishing, with the tourists.'

'He didn't look like a fisherman to me. What's he hanging around for?'

'That's what I wanted to tell you. He thinks that my

father-in-law may not want any publicity about the seal if he can help it. It might spoil the whole political game they're playing, the whole point of the thing for them.'

'He may be shit out of luck. I'm investigating a homicide, not playing games with a by-election.'

'That's what I told him. Anyway, he's hoping that you'll find this guy quickly so they can keep the story of the seal out of it and still play it as they had hoped. Had any leads?'

'What is this? I'm supposed to explain the investigation to you so you can report back to them? I've got some leads, sure, but I'll be goddamned if I have to tell you about them.'

Salter held up his hand. 'I'm not here on a mission. All I wanted to tell you is what is in this guy's head.'

'Does Montagu agree?'

'He hasn't spoken to Montagu yet.'

'That's the point. It's Callendar's idea. So why does *Callendar* want it kept secret?'

'He says that if you publicize the loss of the seal, then it will disappear, because whoever has it will get rid of it.'

'You think that's his real reason? It's just as likely to appear, isn't it? I don't trust the bastard. I'm going to advertise. See what happens.'

Salter nodded. 'Can I talk to my father-in-law first? Just to keep him posted?'

Croll considered for a few moments. 'When do you plan to do that?'

'Right now. This morning.'

'All right. Talk to him. As his son-in-law. Tomorrow morning I'll make up my own mind. Okay?'

'Sure.' Salter was enjoying himself a lot more than he would be looking for clams, and he was eager to demonstrate to Croll that he was a useful ear. But if Croll thought he was getting into the act in any way, he would find himself watching afternoon television with Sheila. 'By the way,' he said. 'I met a guy who offered to sell me some moonshine. Is there that much of it about?'

'What did he ask for it?'

'Fifty dollars a gallon.'

'That's the right price. Yeah, there's a lot of it about. What the hell do they expect? The politicians, I mean. There are thirteen liquor stores on the Island, but some of these people live thirty or forty miles away from the nearest one. There are no beer parlours. It's a classic situation. We've got the strongest temperance movement in Canada. We've also got the highest incidence of alcoholism. I'd say the two were connected, wouldn't you? There's more drunken driving per head of population than there is even in the Northwest territories, where I once laid a charge against a trapper for being drunk in charge of a dog team. I was pretty new, then. Who offered it to you?'

Salter shook his head. 'I'm on holiday. Remember?'

'I've already got my eye on him. Tell him from us that if he gets caught again, he'll wind up in Sleepy Hollow.'

'You know who it is?'

'Sure. Joe. Your fisherman pal. Look, Charlie, when Elton was killed we checked up on just about everybody on the North Shore, knocked on every door, asked the computer to tell us who was the most likely. When Joe's name cropped up I remembered meeting him with you. We've had him once for simple possession. He got away with a fine, but he won't next time. He was probably delivering to Elton that morning. I should have checked the truck.'

'You'll have to find out for yourself. But I'll pass on this much. It wasn't Joe.'

'Really? Did you buy any?'

'No. We get ours from Charlottetown.'

Croll laughed. 'Okay. Stay in touch.'

Salter got up to leave. 'By the way,' he said as he reached the door. 'What the hell is Sleepy Hollow?'

'That's the name of the provincial jail. The real name.'

Only in Prince Edward Island, Salter thought.

CHAPTER 7

The talk with Montagu was brief.

'Tell me how these things work,' Montagu said. 'Croll doesn't really know anything yet, does he?'

'No, I don't think so.'

'If he did, he wouldn't be thinking about the seal one way or the other. So he's going to have to try everything, and if advertising for the seal will help him find Clive's killer then he'll have to do it. I'd like a bit of time, though, to get the story ready for the press. I suppose even the CBC might pick it up in one of those little jokey bits they do at the end of the news. Was he thinking of offering a reward?'

'The police don't like to offer money of their own to recover stolen property. I would guess any reward would be up to you.'

Montagu did some arithmetic doodling on a scrap of paper. 'There's no need to say what it's worth, is there? We don't want to be held up for ransom. If a group of private citizens were to offer two thousand—that's still a lot of money for people around here—that's all that needs to be said. All the Press needs to know is that this group of private citizens, including Clive, had planned to present the seal to the Island. We don't have to say how much we paid for it, do we? Letting the news out now won't do the Premier much good, but it won't do him any harm either. Why were we keeping it secret, then? That's easy. We had only just got it authenticated. Yes, I think that'll wash. I'll have to speak to the others, of course, but they'll go along. Would you mind being messenger boy again? Croll seems to trust you. Ask him if I can have until tomorrow morning. Noon, rather.'

So Salter picked up again, and returned to the police station to deliver his message.

'We'll hold it until the first thing the day after tomorrow,' Croll said.

'They'll be very grateful. Thanks.'

'I'll keep my eyes open for any signs.'

'Of the seal?'

'No. Of their gratitude. Okay, then.'

On an impulse, Salter drove next to Callendar's motel. Callendar was not at home, though the clerk confirmed he was still staying there. An easy second impulse took Salter to the harbour where he found Callendar on the dock, watching one of the boats unload its catch. As Salter approached, Callendar broke off from talking to the fishermen and came forward to meet him, smiling as brilliantly as ever.

'Going fishing again?' Salter asked.

'No, no. Just filling in time, chatting to the locals. Any news?'

Salter told him of the decision to publicize the loss of the seal, to offer a reward.

A cloud seemed to pass over Callendar's face. 'I hope that it works,' he said. 'Do you know all the details?'

Salter told him. As he spoke, Callendar's smile re-emerged. 'That sounds all right. Two thousand, eh? That should catch the local mackerel.' He chuckled. 'I might just stay a day or two more to see if anything turns up right away. Your father-in-law called me last night, by the way, to tell me that at least my principal will be compensated. He was a bit surprised to learn how much my commission was, but I don't expect to collect all of that, in the circumstances. My out-of-pocket expenses will do.'

'What if the seal turns up after he pays you off?'

'It's theirs, of course, and they would pay me the balance of the agreement.'

'How much was your commission?'

'If you weren't so well connected, I wouldn't tell you. But since you are—it was fifty per cent.'

Ten thousand. Enough reason for Callendar to hang about.

'Do you think your father-in-law would like some help with the notice? A description of the seal, for instance?'

'He has the picture. But the Press might want your story after the reward is posted.'

'*My* story?' Callendar stared into Salter's face.

'The discovery of the seal, where it was found, how it came to you. That sort of thing.'

'That ought to remain a bit of a mystery, don't you think?' Callendar thought for a few moments. 'I don't mind telling them as much as I've told you, though. You're right. It's a good story. But my client is absolutely firm about his own privacy. I have to protect that.'

'Your client. He's going to wonder a bit, isn't he? When he hears about the theft, I mean, before he's got his money.'

'Oh, I've stayed in touch. I called him last night to reassure him, just in case he hears anything. Not that he has to worry, because I've guaranteed him, as I told you. That's why I'm relieved your people will pay his bill.'

'There's probably no need to involve you at all, is there? Montagu can just play it close to the chest, giving them the same reason you give—the seal was offered by an anonymous dealer, etc., etc.'

Callendar considered this, then shifted his ground slightly in line with a new thought. 'I suppose you're right. But I wouldn't mind being identified as the agent. Useful publicity, and it would take the pressure off your father-in-law, wouldn't it. Tell him to leave a message at the motel if he wants any help.'

Now Salter was inclined to believe Callendar, but before he drove home, he called Croll and recounted the morning's conversations just to keep the Mountie's confidence.

At home a crisis was brewing. Sheila was sitting in the kitchen, staring out of the window, while Annie made lunch. When Salter began to tell the story of his morning, Annie stepped around him impatiently, and he shut up.

The air of strain continued through the meal. Over coffee, Annie said, 'How would you like to teach me to play golf? Or is it strictly a male sport?' She looked at Salter and kept looking at him until he said, 'Sure. Why didn't you ask me before?'

'I thought I wouldn't like it. But you and Angus seem to enjoy it.'

'You want to come, Sheila?' Salter asked.

'No, thanks. I'm bored, but not that bored.'

This offended Salter in several ways at once: on behalf of Annie, who had worked like a traffic cop to entertain her; on his own behalf as the possibly negligent host; and, surprisingly, on behalf of the Island which he felt immediately compelled to defend. Salter now guessed that it was her boredom that was causing the strain. 'You don't come here to be entertained,' he said. 'You come here to rest. Why don't you play tennis, or go down to the yacht club?' He tried to speak jocularly, but the rudeness was real.

'Come off it, Charlie. You were hanging about yourself like a spare general until this murder cropped up. I don't like sailing or tennis any more than you do, and I've had my rest.'

So go back to Toronto, Salter thought. 'What will you do, then?' he asked.

'I'll just stay home and read, if I can find anything to read.'

Annie looked away.

Salter said, 'You want to come, Angus?'

'No, thanks,' the boy replied from the corner of the room where he had been keeping his head down. 'I'll go down to the harbour. See if I can go out with Joe 'n' Eddie.'

'Right.' Salter looked at the clock on the kitchen stove. 'We'll leave in half an hour. Should Angus take the cooler to bring us back some fish?'

'No,' Angus said. 'No more fish. Ever. I'm growing gills.'

Sheila laughed. 'What then, Angus?'

'Hot dogs. Hamburgers. Chili. Spaghetti. Lasagna.' He let his tongue taste the word, saying it twice. 'Lasagna. But no more fish, or clam chowder, or lobsters. Please?'

'Your grandfather remembers that in the 'thirties you could tell the really poor kids because they took lobsters to school for their lunch. The kids from better-off families got boloney sandwiches,' Annie said.

'I know how the poor kids felt. Even mystery meat would be better than lobsters.'

'What's mystery meat?' Sheila asked.

'What we get at school for lunch.' He stood up. 'Would you drop me off, Dad? Unless I can have a car.'

'It's only about four hundred yards away. All right, we'll drop you off and pick you up about four-thirty on our way home. If we're late, walk. Have you got a watch?'

'It's okay. I'll just hang around until you come.'

In the car, after they had deposited Angus, Salter said, 'This is great. I wish you'd asked me before.'

Annie said nothing. Salter looked at her profile and returned to wondering what was going on. Whatever was behind Annie's mood, it did not augur well for a fun afternoon on the links, but at some point she would tell him what it was all about and they could go home.

On the first tee he arranged her feet, then wrapped himself around her from behind as he got her hands placed properly on the club shaft. He explained carefully how to swing, how to keep her head down and the importance of following through. She took a few practice swings, and when he judged she might connect he teed up a ball. 'Now try it,' he said.

Observing rigidly everything he had told her, she brought the club down and hit the ball perfectly square; it soared into the air and ended up a hundred and fifty yards down the fairway. 'Like that?'

Salter shouted with joy. He had been expecting at best that she might top the ball twenty feet, or perhaps miss it entirely. Now on the first swing of her life she had managed a near-perfect hit. She would not do it again that day, or even for weeks, but that she had done it once meant she would now be totally hooked on the game. 'Terrific,' he said.

She smiled. 'Did I do it right?'

'Perfect.' He teed up and drove off, managing a reasonable drive, and they walked down the fairway together. After that she hacked and slashed her way through the first four holes, only occasionally getting the ball into the air, but her first drive was her guarantee that all the shots that followed were errors to be ignored. On the fourth hole she began experimenting, rearranging her hands and feet, qualifying his advice with her experience. On the fifth tee she missed the ball so badly that Salter once more placed his hands on hers from behind to straighten her out. He kept his arms around her minimally longer than was necessary, and she turned her head around. 'Is this how you planned to teach Eleanor?' she asked.

He bumped her gently from behind. 'Let's go home,' he said. 'It's starting to rain.'

Annie shook her head. 'Sheila's there.'

'Then let's go to a motel.' He held his breath. If her new mood was not secure, then paying her sexual compliments was a risky business.

Again Annie shook her head. 'We'd have to go to Souris, and even there someone would recognize me.'

'Who cares? We're married.'

'*I* care. I'm uptight, tight-assed, afraid to express myself. Okay?'

'So what, then?' This was a new Annie, interesting, but liable to explode. To be handled with care.

She put her club back in the bag and started back to the clubhouse. 'I'll show you,' she said.

Back in the car she directed Salter along Highway 6 to where it met the Kings Byway, and from there to Charlottetown.

'Keep going?' he asked, as they drove along St Peter's Road.

'Keep going.'

They crossed Charlottetown and turned right along the North River Road. 'Are we going to your folks' place?'

'Not quite. Left here. Now right.'

'We're going to the family cottage. Right?'

She said nothing, just nodded, and he pulled up outside. 'Getting out, are we?'

'Lock the car.'

They found the key in the woodshed and she led the way inside and up to their old bedroom. 'It's the WASP in me,' she said. 'I can't fuck in public. I never could.' She shucked off her clothes and climbed in under the covers.

Salter kicked off his clothes and fumbled into her embrace, awkwardly, like a teenager, but there had been too much wonder, and he was finding the scene intensely erotic. In seconds, he was still.

He collected himself and lay back. 'Not much, was it?'

'More than you think. We've hardly spoken to each other for ten days. It's like the first time, and you can never expect much the first time.'

'Is that what's going on?'

'That's what's going on. I just wanted you back for a couple of hours before I go on duty again. I got what I needed.'

Salter waited for more guidance.

She turned and snuggled into him, taking possession like a child. And then, 'Do you *like* Sheila?' she asked.

'What? I can't stand the bloody woman, you know that. What kind of question is that?'

'I was just wondering if that was it, or whether you found her attractive and were covering up.'

'Jesus Christ. Now you're talking like her!'

'Am I? She likes you all right. She can't keep her eyes off you. And she keeps telling me about her needs. "I have needs, too" she keeps saying, rolling her bloody eyes.'

'And that's it?'

'That's all. I just wanted you to make a pass at me and talk to me. That surprise you? Age cannot wither me nor custom stale my something variety, as my mother would say.'

They were silent for a while and Salter dozed off for a few moments. This, though, was no more than the dissolving of some of his anxieties as he relaxed, and he was prevented from falling asleep by the surprising discovery of finding himself for the first time in years stirred to amorous life twice within an hour. This time he loved at her command, secure of infinity as she reached for her pleasure. When he next looked at her she was already asleep.

He lay back and closed his eyes. After a while, he felt her tickling him. 'We'd better go and get Angus, hadn't we?' she said.

'It's only three-thirty. We've got this room booked for another hour.'

'What would you do if I called your bluff?'

'Who knows? Give me one of your feet, and let's see what happens.' She wriggled away. 'We'd better go back to the harbour so we can pretend we've been fishing. We can say who was on the boat with us.'

Salter watched her climb out of bed, moved to foolishness by her nakedness and by how little it seemed to him she had changed in the twenty years since he had found her on the Island. He leaned over and swept his hand from the nape of her neck down her back, tucking it firmly under her bottom where she sat on the edge of the bed. 'Sorry,' he said.

She looked at him over her shoulder. 'What?'

'Sorry. You've been having a hard time. I should have realized. Sheila's really got you down, hasn't she?'

She swung her legs back on the bed and rolled into him, sliding herself inside his arm. 'It isn't all Sheila,' she said.

'It's me, too?'

'Sometimes you make it harder for me than it need be, do you know that?'

'What can I do? It's your family. I'm an outsider here.'

'So you *do* know. Yes, it's *my* family we come to see, and every time you make that pretty plain.'

Salter felt the glumness that comes with the consciousness of having been a boor. 'What can I do?' he asked.

'Well, you could look after Sheila a bit. I know she gets on your nerves, but if you'd take her off my hands sometimes, *I* could visit the people I haven't seen and *you* wouldn't have to come.'

'You trust me with her?' Salter gave her bottom a squeeze.

'No, but maybe that's a part of being a good host, too. Besides—' she leaned away from him and looked down— 'you don't look much of a threat right now.'

He made a lunge at her but she was already gone, across the bed and into the bathroom. Salter sat on the edge of the bed, stroking his chest, feeling smug and happy.

CHAPTER 8

The tourist boats had not returned, so Salter was surprised to see Callendar sitting on the harbour wall.

'What happened, Mr Callendar? I thought you were going fishing?'

Callendar, who had watched Salter and Annie approach, showed his teeth. 'I felt too idle. It seemed an afternoon for sitting in the sun, rather. No news yet, of course?'

'Not that I know of.' Salter introduced Annie to Callendar. 'We've been out all afternoon.'

Annie saw someone she knew along the wharf and excused herself. Salter propped himself on the wall and picked up the newspaper that Callendar had been carrying. 'Nothing about the seal yet,' he remarked. 'If they print your picture you'll be famous, around here.'

'I don't think so, do you? I think that only happens in books, unless you're Prince Charles. In books it happens all the time, doesn't it? You know, "She realized that the man getting on at the other end of the train was the man whose picture she had seen three months before in the Swiss newspaper, wanted for murder." In real life you might remember someone's picture if he were Chinese, say, with one ear missing. Otherwise the chance is very slim, I think. And those identikits are surely useless. They always look as thought they had been pasted together out of bits of people one knows, but the result is never a human being. Has anyone ever been identified from an identikit, Inspector? Perhaps they work negatively, though, eliminating the cranks who inform on everybody.'

Salter listened to Callendar burble on, not feeling called on to reply. Two fishing-boats appeared in the mouth of the harbour. They watched them tie up and disembark their load of tourists, each with three or four mackerel in a plastic bag. Salter looked around for Annie among the handful of sightseers and his eye caught and recognized one man leaning over the harbour wall, watching the boats unload. 'Excuse me a moment,' Salter said and walked over to the warehouse where, from a window inside, he confirmed that the man was, in fact, watching Callendar. When he rejoined Callendar, Annie had arrived and he offered the dealer a lift back to his motel.

Callendar refused. 'This is a pleasanter place to kill time than my room. I'll just sit here for a bit and walk back.'

'It's starting to rain again,' Salter pointed out.

'A scotch mist.' Callendar waved his hand dismissively. 'Not enough to take away from the charm of the scene. Adds to it, rather. Like looking at a pretty woman through a screen door.'

'It's two miles.'

'Then perhaps I'll jog,' Callendar said, a small edge of "why-don't-you-shut-up-and-go-away" creeping into his voice, past the smiling teeth. 'Don't worry about me. I'll find a way.'

Salter took the hint, and joined Annie in the car. 'Who were you talking to?' he asked.

'Fred Sturrock. He works for Dad in the winter. We've known him for years. He thought you'd been brought in from Toronto to help out the local police. Like Scotland Yard.'

'Christ, I hope Croll doesn't hear that. You were talking about Elton, were you?'

'They all were. Their theory is that it was one of the tourists.'

Angus was helping Eddie tidy up the boat and Salter leaned out of the car and called to him.

'Catch anything?' he asked when the boy arrived.

Angus launched into an excited and tedious description of the big cod he had nearly brought in, a description which lasted them up to the cottage, where they found Sheila entertaining Jim Brady in the kitchen. Brady had arrived with the butcher's block, and accepted an invitation for coffee while he waited for Salter to help him unload it. When Salter and Annie walked in, he was in the middle of a story of a time he had spent in the high Arctic, working on the D.E.W. line. He broke off and stood up as he was interrupted by Annie's enthusiasm for her chopping block. The two men brought it into the house and Salter paid Brady off.

Salter felt the pressure of women's eyes on him and he looked around to find both of them watching him expectantly. Was there something he was supposed to tell Brady?

He stared back at Annie, waiting for a clue.

'Perhaps Mr Brady would like a beer,' Annie said.

'Oh, right,' Salter said. 'You finished for the day, Jim? Got time?'

'Sure.' Brady sat down again and Salter got some beer out of the fridge. Sheila accepted, too, but Annie excused herself and disappeared, and the three of them sat around the kitchen table.

'What do you think of Jim's T-shirt?' Sheila asked. 'Isn't it terrific?'

Printed across the front of Brady's chest was the legend, WHERE THE HELL *IS* TORONTO? Salter had seen it immediately and decided to ignore it, but now he was obliged to smile. 'Where did you pick that up? Montreal?' he asked.

Brady grinned and pulled the shirt tight over his chest and looked down at himself. 'One of my customers gave it to me. A baseball fan. He bought it outside Yankee Stadium during the series.'

'He knows now, doesn't he?' And then, 'Finished the table for Miss Vail?' he asked, changing the subject to the first thing that came into his head.

'Oh, yeah. But she wants me to put a shelf beside it, and do a couple other little jobs.' Brady looked at his watch. 'Maybe I'll call in on her now.'

'Good, thought Salter. Off you go, then. A silence grew as Sheila waited for Salter to make some more conversation. Salter, however, felt that one beer and one conversational gambit were enough.

Brady lowered the contents of the bottle down his throat and put the bottle on the table, totally at his ease.

'Another beer, Jim?' Sheila asked.

For a moment Salter thought Brady was going to accept, but the carpenter shook his head and stood up. 'I'll take a rain check,' he said, nodding to Salter.

Like hell, thought Salter.

'When did he get here?' Salter asked when Brady was gone.

'Hours ago. Just after you left. He's a really interesting character. He's done everything. We were just talking about the murder.' Her enthusiasm for Brady was startling.

Salter said, 'Did he have any theories about who did it?'

'Oh no, we were just talking about it.' Sheila gathered herself and launched forward on a fresh wave of enthusiasm. 'He's taking me to an auction on Monday. He buys things and resells them after he's fixed them up. He's really fascinating.'

Annie, entering the room at this point, said, 'But I thought we were going to Tignish on Monday. Weren't we?'

'Do you mind if we do that another day? This auction is pretty special, Jim says. A lot of the furniture was made here on the Island in the nineteenth century.'

'Mind?' Annie repeated later when she was alone with Salter. 'Why should I mind? I've been racking my brains trying to think of ways to entertain the woman. Jim Brady will give me a holiday.'

'I didn't know she was interested in antiques.'

'Don't be silly, it's Brady she's interested in. He's the nearest thing to a gipsy you can get these days. He's a— what's the word, not a gamekeeper, that's too obvious— he's a tinker. He represents mystery, romance, stuff like that. He smells of sulphur, too.'

'Brady? He's a second-hand junk-dealer from Saskatchewan. He's out here dodging his alimony payments.'

'How do you know that?'

'I'm just guessing.'

Annie considered this. 'It's the same thing, probably. Anyway, if he keeps her occupied for the next ten days I don't mind if he's wanted for bigamy in South Porcupine. Try not to feel threatened by him. I'm still in your cave.' She disappeared, grinning.

*

The next morning the group assembled in Montagu's office and prepared the announcement. They prepared two: the reward notice, and the story of the discovery of the seal for the Press. The reward notice simply stated that a $2000 reward was offered for information leading to the recovery of the Great Silver Seal, believed stolen recently from a private home on the Island. There was a picture of the seal, reproduced from that found in Elton's drawer, and a description of its size and weight.

The Press story gave an account of how the seal had come to light in Marblehead and been offered to a dealer in Toronto. A group of businessmen who were interested in the Island's history had arranged to buy the seal, at no cost to the government, and present it to the Historical Society. The arrangements had been kept confidential until the transaction was complete so that (here a small fiction was constructed) a surprise announcement could be made on the Island's birthday. The report ended with the information that a Mr Barry Callendar was the Toronto dealer who had negotiated the sale, and he was now on the Island assisting the police.

'Are you sure you want that in, Barry?' Montagu asked. 'There's no real need to drag you in at all, as far as I can see.'

'Just ego-satisfaction,' Callendar said. 'Pure vanity. If we don't get the seal back, at least I'll have a little clipping for my scrapbook. Besides, it will do me no harm in the trade. Word will get around that I'm the top specialist in arcane Maritime memorabilia.' He flashed his teeth round the room.

'So be it. You can have these, Sergeant. To be released at what—nine a.m. tomorrow?'

The group broke up and Salter collected Callendar to take him back to his motel.

'How much longer will you be staying here?' Salter asked.

'Another day, I think. Just in case there's an immediate

response. I thought I'd try a bit of fishing again from somewhere else on the Island. I enjoyed our afternoon together. Do you know of any other harbours where they take out tourists? Nearby, I mean.'

'There are a couple of boats that go out of Covehead Bay, I think. You want to borrow the raincoat and boots?'

'Yes, I should, shouldn't I. That's very kind.'

'They're still in the trunk. I'll dig them out at the motel.'

When he deposited Callendar at the door of the motel and handed over the fishing.clothes, he said, out of pity for the man, 'Would you like some company?'

'Oh no. You mustn't bother with me. I'll enjoy myself on my own. Thanks so much. Now I must telephone Toronto to let them know I haven't drowned.'

The story appeared the following day, along with the reward notice. It made a huge splash locally, and even, as predicted, a tiny ploomp in the waters of the national press, the first Prince Edward Island Story for a long time that was not concerned with Anne of Green Gables, lobsters, or potatoes. There were pictures of the seal and, in the local press, of Barry Callendar. When the Opposition realized that the Premier had known what was going on they raised a vote-getting fuss about the fact that a precious Island legacy had been lost because of the partisan and irresponsible behaviour of the government which had not moved to protect the seal as soon as they knew of its existence. The Premier responded by accusing the Opposition of making cheap political mileage out of what had been planned as a birthday surprise for the Islanders, nothing to do with the election. And Staff Sergeant Croll said he had a number of leads.

It seemed to Annie inhospitable to leave Sheila on her own for the weekend while they attended the wedding in Halifax. She assured Sheila that she would be welcome at the feast, but Sheila urged them to forget about her and insisted she was looking forward to being on her own for a couple of days. On the Friday beforehand, Annie had to go to Charlottetown to pick up Seth who was going with them to the wedding, Angus was off to the harbour to join Joe 'n' Eddie, and Annie urged Salter to find an outing to take Sheila on.

'You think I'll be safe?' Salter asked.

'Haven't you noticed? She's gone off you lately.'

'I never noticed she was on. All right. I'll think of something.'

He spent a few minutes with the local paper and found what he wanted. Over lunch, he said to Sheila, 'How about taking a look at the Tyne Valley Festival this afternoon?'

'Oh yes,' Annie said. 'Is it on? You'll love it, Sheila.'

'Festival of what?' Sheila asked.

'Oysters, mainly,' Salter said. 'Raw, fried, stewed. All you can eat. We could drive out around Mapleque Bay and come home across country.'

Sheila said, 'That's it? A drive to Tyne Valley to eat oysters?' She considered the suggestion with a raised eyebrow.

'Oh, there's more than oysters,' Annie said. 'It's a whole festival. You remember last year, Charlie? Those fiddlers?'

'Right. They have a fiddling competition,' Salter explained to Sheila. 'A guy named Arsenault wins it every year.'

'The same man, year after year?'

'No, all the fiddlers are named Arsenault, so it's always won by a man named Arsenault.'

'I won't come if you are going to make jokes like that all afternoon.'

Salter, noting her good mood, felt more cheerful himself about the prospect. 'And if we're lucky,' he said, 'We'll see the step-dancing. The step-dancers are all called Gallant. They're terrific. Did you ever see step-dancing in New Brunswick? They just stand and smile. From the waist up they don't move a muscle—they look as if they are having their chests X-rayed. But their feet fly about in this fantastic dance. Last year there were two sisters doing it together. They were terrific.'

'What should I wear, Annie?'

And so it was agreed.

In the event they took one look at the tourist traffic crawling along the coast through the park and decided to go inland, through Kensington. Salter, though primarily still doing his duty to a guest he didn't like much, felt some low-level twinges of curiosity about her. Sheila had been much less of a strain these last couple of days and he wondered how much of that was a change in her, and if so, why, and how much he and Annie were projecting out of the tiny honeymoon they were having. He also wondered, if he took her for a stroll among the dunes, whether she would jump him, and if she did what he would do about it.

They reached Tyne Valley and asked their way to the festival site, surprised at the absence of crowds. When they arrived at the fairgrounds they saw why. Today was Friday; the festival began the next day.

'Now what?' she asked.

Salter got the map out of the glove compartment. 'We could drive out to Gillis Point,' he said. 'It's probably a dirt road. Be pretty quiet. We could go for a walk along the cliff, if there is one.'

She looked at the map over his shoulder. 'No, thanks,' she said. 'Let's go back around the coast. It's nice just driving around.'

Then, as they passed through MacDougall, she said, 'Look, there's a farm auction. Lets see what it's like.'

The signs directed them along the back roads to the farm that was being sold. There the yard was filled with a crowd, mostly tourists with a sprinkling of local farmers and house-wives. The farm machinery had already been sold and the auctioneer was beginning on the furniture. It was a real auction: much of the stuff was rubbish—a formica and chrome kitchen set dating from the 'fifties, the seats repaired with electrical tape; a chesterfield upholstered in tweed and Lurex of the kind Salter remembered from his childhood but some of it, several bureaus and side tables and many of the smaller items, had been new before the First World War.

'Look at that washbowl,' Sheila said, catching fire at the possibility of picking up something that would decorate her Toronto apartment. 'And look, isn't that an apple-corer? I've been looking for one of those.'

She began to push to the front of the crowd and Salter let her go and wandered off to the edge of the yard. By the gate an old man with a face like a warty apple was sitting on a kitchen chair watching the crowd arrive. He looked at Salter. 'You from around here?' he asked, then shook his head. 'I never seen you before.'

Salter said, 'I live in Marlow.'

'You're not from there, either,' the old man said.

'No, I'm from Toronto.'

The old man grunted. 'Like everybody else here, seems like. What do they want with stuff like this?'

'They're looking for antiques, bargains, I guess.'

The old man looked around. 'That right? I'm an antique meself. No bargain, though.'

Then Salter realized from the old man's attitude, his proprietorial air, that he was talking to the owner. 'This your place?' he asked.

'Was,' the old man said. 'Has been for forty years. Was my wife's father's before that, and his father's before that. I don't know who had it before that. They're all dead now, though. Just me left.'

'Now for this little rocking-crib,' the auctioneer called. 'How much? Twenty dollars?'

'It would make a lovely planter,' someone said, from the crowd.

'I made that crib meself,' the old man said. 'For me

daughter. I'm going to live with her now.'

'Is she here? Doesn't she want any of this stuff?'

'No. She's got all new stuff, hasn't she?' The old man turned to watch the people who were leaving already, clutching their purchases, and Salter, feeling dismissed, moved off to look for Sheila. When he found her she was deep in conversation with someone whose back looked familiar. Salter called to her, and she turned round.

'Look who I've found,' she called back. It was Jim Brady.

'See any bargains, Jim?' Salter asked when he had caught up to them.

'I'm waiting for that rocking-chair,' Brady said, pointing. 'I've got a customer who wants one.'

'I've got my apple-corer,' Sheila said, holding up the piece of rusted tin. 'Two dollars. Jim said it was cheap.'

Salter wanted to go home. 'That it, then?' he asked her. 'Shall we be off now?'

'Oh no.' Sheila was dismayed. 'Oh no. I want to see the rest of it. Jim's been explaining to me what to bid on. Oh no, I don't want to go home yet.'

Salter looked around the yard. The crowd was thinning but there were plenty of odds and ends yet to sell. It would, he figured, be another hour at least.

Brady said, 'I'll bring her home if you want to get off.'

Salter looked at Sheila, who looked back at him brightly, leaving him wondering what he was supposed to do. She was his guest, he decided. 'That's okay, Jim,' he said. 'I'll wait. I'll meet you by the car when it's over.' He walked out to the gate, to the old man who watched him coming.

'You gotta wait for your lady?' the old man said. 'I seen you talking to her.'

'That's right. She wants to stay to the end.'

The old man stood up. 'Come on along of me,' he said, and gave his body a corkscrew twist that ended with a beckoning gesture from his head. Salter followed where he led, out past the farmhouse to the barn. On the way, with more corkscrew gestures from the old man, they collected two other men who were standing in the background. Inside the barn, the old man said, 'That's enough of that. You get her out, Ben.'

One of the men shifted a bale of hay and produced a case of beer. He took out four bottles, flipping the caps off against the hasp of the barn door. They dragged two more bales out and the four men sat down and made themselves comfortable, the noise of the auctioneer faint in the distance. Salter felt honoured and tried to sing for his supper by making conversation, but after a few polite remarks the others ignored him, except to give him another beer, while they talked about auctions. The two men were neighbours of the owner, and they talked, often incomprehensibly to Salter, of the difficulty of making a farm pay any more, of the lucky ones whose farms ran down to the sea and were therefore valuable as summer homes to 'fellas from Toronto and Boston'. One of the men asked the owner if he was selling his hay. 'Sold it,' the old man said. 'They want it at the festival. They're picking it up tonight.' After two beers the three of them stood up as if by signal, and Salter scrambled to his feet and helped them cache the beer and put the hay bales back in place.

He walked back to the gate with the old man and thanked him for the beer, wondering if he should offer to pay him. The old man said, 'You looked thirsty, young fella. There's your lady now,' and pointed to Sheila and Brady who were walking towards them. As well as her apple-corer, Sheila was now carrying a bread mould and a tin candle-holder. Salter suddenly did not want them all to meet, and he nodded to the old man and intercepted the other two to head them through the gate.

'Who was that?' Sheila asked. 'He looked like Rip Van Winkle.'

'The owner,' Salter said, and then to avoid anything

further, he said to Brady, 'Did you get your rocking-chair?'
'It's in the truck.'
'He got it for almost nothing. Didn't you, Jim?'
'Good,' Salter said. 'Let's go home.'

That night, talking to Annie in bed, he tried to explain to her what had happened that afternoon.

'I'm not putting anyone down,' he said. 'Okay? But this is what happened. When we got there, Sheila started in right away about some washbowl she saw. She didn't buy it so I suppose they are in big demand. That was enough to hook her, though, and she really got into it. Then we met Jim Brady, on business, looking to buy anything he could sell. All round us were these tourists picking over this pile of stuff, just like Sheila, having a ball, going to a farm auction. Then I ran into this old guy sitting on a chair by the gate, just watching like a security guard. You know who he was? He was the owner, for Chrissake. They were selling his furniture and his machinery, even his hay—everything including the house and land he'd had for three generations, at least. A prickly old bugger he looked, just like my dad. Then he took me out to the barn and offered me a beer, and there I was listening to these three farmers talking about the best time to have an auction. In the summer they said, when the tourists are around. These people have lived there as long as your family's been on the Island. This guy's whole life was stacked up in the yard. You know, from what I heard the real way of life on the Island is selling at auctions —not farming or fishing. Auctions.'

'That's how Dad got this house.'

'I know. I said I wasn't putting anybody down. Anyway the woman who owned this place died, didn't she? This old guy was still sitting there, watching.'

'Did Jim buy anything?' Annie said after a while.

'Just a rocking-chair.' Salter turned over and settled himself to sleep. 'Cheap, too,' he added.

CHAPTER 9

Salter had no idea of what to expect at the wedding. His experience of weddings was small but varied. His favourite had been a Ukrainian one in Winnipeg twenty-five years before when, after a mysterious ceremony in a Greek Orthodox church, there had been a huge reception and dance at a Ukrainian social club with superb food and unlimited drink. Legend had it that at one stage of the evening everyone was supposed to dance with the bride and pin money on her dress and Salter had armed himself with a twenty-dollar bill and a pin, but the reality turned out to be a ceremony half way through the evening when the guests lined up to present an envelope to the happy couple. The economics seemed to be that the bride's father spent a fortune on the wedding and the bride got it all back, in cash, at the reception. A very sensible arrangement, Salter thought. The wedding, or rather the party afterwards, had gone on for three days.

The others he had attended, Anglican, City Hall and, in one case, Salvation Army, had lasted only a couple of hours. His own had been tiny. Out of consideration for the fact that Salter could not expect his friends to travel from Toronto to Charlottetown (even his father had refused to come) Annie had kept a tight grip on the arrangements, turning it into a small country wedding with only twenty guests, thus creating rumours among the mainland relatives that Annie was eight months pregnant and that Salter was black.

This wedding was a gathering of two clans from three provinces: the Montagus—the groom's family—and the McGlones who, like the Montagus, had settled in Nova Scotia in the early nineteenth century and were now spread out from Cape Breton Island to Lunenberg, with small branches in every major town. The headquarters, the largest concentration of the Clan McGlone, was still Halifax, and here Annie's second cousin had courted his bride, and here the two hundred members of both families assembled for the rites.

The Salters joined the Montagus at Charlottetown airport to catch the morning plane. The Island contingent, including Annie's brothers and their children, half-filled the plane and for them the wedding began in the *Nova Scotian* in Halifax where Annie's father had booked a suite of rooms to accommodate them all for the night and laid on a lunch for about forty of his kinsmen before the wedding.

The ceremony was familiar enough for Salter to enjoy and even lose himself in. He had not been inside a church for fifteen years, but his upbringing in Cabbagetown had been Anglican and included Sunday school and he remembered all the hymns. The bride looked as happy as brides do, dressed in white with a tartan sash. The groom, as well as several of the guests, wore a kilt, and Salter entertained himself by thinking about what his father, the working-class Anglo-Saxon who hated Scots as well as all other races and classes not his own, would have made of it. A blessing in Gaelic would have provided the old man's prejudices with enough fuel to last the evening.

From the church they were driven to the reception which was held in what looked to Salter like the Lieutenant-Governor's mansion, but he was told was the residence of the bride's family. During the initial drinks, Salter found himself a well-regarded stranger from Toronto, Annie's husband, the policeman, of whom they had heard. Most of his connections by marriage he had never met and for at least an hour he got an oral genealogy of the clan, of Annie's place in it, and of its history, along with comical and tender anecdotes of Annie's childhood. Everyone worked to make him welcome, and, more discreetly, to find out about him, to size him up. The story of the loss of the seal, of Montagu's involvement with it, and of Salter's connection with the investigation was widely known, and it gave everyone something to talk to him about. Salter spent some time lecturing to small groups on how crime and the law worked, feeling slightly silly whenever Annie was by, but generally happy that the topic allowed him to do his share of making conversation. Annie hovered like a butterfly, eager herself to talk to all the people she had not seen for years, but circling back continuously to make sure Salter was all right.

Then, beginning at some point during the toasts, and lasting through the first part of the drinking afterwards, Salter found himself outside of things as the families relaxed and retold all those private jokes and stories that successful large families accumulate. There were a lot of speeches after the dinner, mostly incomprehensible to Salter because of the in-jokes which by now no one was bothering to explain to him. There was a toast in Gaelic which everyone except Salter understood, and a Latin grace which took nobody else by surprise. After dinner they moved to another huge room for the drinking and dancing, and Salter found a quiet corner to drink in. He assured Annie he was fine, really, and she abandoned him as he settled down to watch. He was intrigued to see that his sons were completely at home, not only because they knew their cousins from the sailing club, but because they belonged to the clan by birth. Were they his sons, really, he wondered, the sons of Charlie Salter from Hogtown? His musings were interrupted by Montagu himself who sat down next to him, ostensibly to make sure he was having a good time. But after the initial courtesies, he said, 'By the way, when we get back on Monday I've arranged a meeting with Croll in my office. Could you drop by? At ten?'

'What about?' Salter asked. The seal, the homicide, were not nearly as important as the wedding at that moment. They could wait.

'Croll wants to give the Press the full story. I'd like to talk it over first.'

'He doesn't have to ask your permission, Robert. He's trying to find a killer.'

'Of course. I know that. But I'd like to know what he's thinking. Have you spoken to him lately?'

'No, but I know what he must be thinking. You want to hear about it?'

'If it's not—well, yes, I would.'

Salter found it pleasant to think that Montagu believed he and Croll were sharing as professionals ideas that Montagu was not privy to. He accepted a drink from a waiter and began. 'I think Croll is working on the possibility that Callendar set the whole thing up and if he can prove it he might get a lead on his homicide. He's checked out Marblehead to find this dealer and no one has ever heard of the seal, not the dealers, not the galleries—there's been no sign of it.'

'According to Callendar it's a private dealer, someone who wants to remain anonymous so why would anyone have heard of it?'

'Think about it for a minute. First of all he must be known to someone or how would he deal? Then think about the Great Silver Seal of Prince Edward Island.' Here Salter's voice took on a mocking edge, as he spoke on Croll's behalf. 'How many people would know it if they fell over it? You would, maybe, but how many others even know what it looks like? How many Americans, for God's sake? So this private collector comes across a piece of metal somewhere in Massachusetts and says, Aha! The Great Silver Seal of Prince Edward Island, lost in 1775? It's bullshit, Elmer, and I say don't eat it. That's what Croll thinks.'

'A regular visitor who happens to be a collector might come across it on the Island and recognize it.'

'A bit remote, isn't it? Someone on the Island had to find it first. Someone found that thing on the Island, took it to

Toronto and cooked up a little scheme with Callendar. That's the likeliest, and that's what Croll thinks. Has anyone seen even a picture of the thing except the one we found at Elton's?'

Montagu sipped his drink and called greetings to a couple on the floor. Salter felt that he was getting a glimpse of the true life of all wheeler-dealers like Montagu. Whenever you see them at the yacht club or wherever, looking as if they are chatting about their begonias, all the time they are working on a deal, like Montagu now. Salter waved at Annie, waiting for Montagu to continue.

'What are the other possibilities?'

'Once you start, they're endless,' Salter said, thinking: Nor do I want to think about them now. I'm at a wedding.

'You know,' Montagu said. 'I don't care much if Callendar is his own principal. It's all the same to me who is behind him. The seal is worth twenty thousand to us.'

'It makes a difference to Croll, though.' Salter allowed this reminder to sink in, of the difference between his interests and Croll's. Before Montagu could reply, Annie appeared, looking irritated as she guessed what they were talking about. 'This is a party,' she said. 'Come and dance.'

'I thought you'd never ask,' Salter said as he led her into the middle of the room.

A dixieland band was playing and the floor was full of people dancing in the manner of twenty years ago. Salter, diffidently at first, then with enthusiasm, swung Annie around the floor, wondering why they didn't do this more often. After two sets they took a break, sweaty and grinning, and the next stage of the party took hold. Some of the relatives had recovered their dislike of each other, and once they had heard each other's news they regrouped in search of better drinking companions. Now Salter found himself sought after by kindred spirits and before long he had become a bosom pal of four or five people who seemed to him to be the cream of humanity. The party rolled towards the dawn, and the call came for a reel, but not all the liquor in Nova Scotia could make Salter join in that and he retired to his chair to watch Annie twirl around with her kin. He had had a good wedding. And the conversation with Montagu had activated something in his mind, putting words to a question that had lain there dormant since he had been in Elton's house. He decided, when he got back to have a look again at the picture of the seal. No need to tell Croll yet.

On Sunday morning the parents of the groom arranged a gigantic brunch for the out-of-town guests at a yacht club; after which the Salters caught the afternoon plane back to Charlottetown. At home they found Sheila contentedly reading a book on the porch, just waiting for their arrival to start cooking the dinner she had planned. Salter mouthed his surprise to Annie who shut him up with a gesture. When Annie asked Sheila how she had spent her time she got a shrug and a smile and the answer that she had just 'puttered around'. 'Jim Brady came by yesterday to remind me we're going to an auction tomorrow. Except for him I didn't see anybody,' she said.

'Did it rain on Saturday?' Annie asked. 'We had some showers in Halifax.'

'Poured all day,' Sheila said. 'I hope the bride didn't get wet. Now put your feet up. I've got the dinner all worked out.'

'Let's do it again,' Salter said in bed that night. 'Next weekend.'

When Salter arrived in Montagu's office on Monday morning, Croll was already waiting.

'Any sign of the seal?' Montagu asked when they were settled. He looked at Salter who was staring out the window. 'I realize the homicide is the important thing.'

'Nothing,' Croll said. 'Not a thing.'

There was a long pause.

'Charlie tells me you are working on the assumption that Callendar is a swindler,' Montagu said.

'I said that's the assumption *I* would work on,' Salter said.

'It's our training,' Croll said. 'The law assumes everyone is innocent. We don't.'

'Any leads on the robber?' Salter asked.

'We've picked up a trace of a guy who's been selling stuff for about three months now. He tried a few of the regular dealers in Toronto a couple of months ago but they wouldn't touch him.'

'An Islander?'

'No one said he was covered in red dust. They remember that he was dark, is all. He wasn't wearing a sou'wester and rubber boots either, but one of the dealers had the impression that he was from the Maritimes. He can't remember why.'

'But they haven't seen him lately.'

'The best we have is that two dealers think they saw him once.'

'What was he trying to sell?' Salter asked.

'Bits and pieces, they said. One of them remembers an antique silver cup, the kind they used to measure our spirits. There was one on our list, stolen from the Smallwoods' place.'

'Is Fehely having any luck?'

'He hasn't found a ring of cab-drivers yet. He's working on this new tack, looking for a guy who goes to Toronto regularly. Someone who might be selling the stuff. He's trying to check on people who used the ferry a lot this summer.'

'Why is Callendar staying around?' Montagu asked.

Croll slapped the arm of his chair. 'That's the one *I've* been asking. Just protecting his interests maybe? So he can collect his money when the seal turns up? But it could be he's been trying to keep a lid on the story. Suppose someone sold him the seal for peanuts? So far the reward is two thousand, which may not bother the guy too much, but if he hears that Callendar is getting twenty thousand he may come after him with a filleting knife. That's why I wanted to see you this morning. I want to give the full story to the Press, including the price.'

'But Callendar may get hurt,' Montagu protested. 'If he's swindled one of the local people, I mean.'

'I wouldn't worry too much about that,' Salter said. 'Brian is looking after Callendar.'

Croll looked at him, and Salter laughed. 'I was down at the harbour the other day, talking to Callendar. I wondered who that clean-looking fisherman was who was propping up the wall. Nice haircut, too.'

Croll smiled slightly. 'He reported that two suspicious-looking characters had approached Callendar. A man and a woman.'

'That was me and Annie.' Salter turned to Montagu. 'So don't worry about Callendar. He's under protective surveillance. He's the only one who doesn't know it.'

'All right. The papers are on to the whole story anyway. They are asking me about the connection between the seal and Clive's death.'

'So tell 'em.' Croll said. 'Maybe we can smoke this guy out.'

'I wouldn't wait around if I were Callendar,' Montagu said. 'He doesn't know you're protecting him.'

'There's another possibility,' Croll said after a few moments. 'Callendar may be hanging around hoping the killer will approach him. He spent the weekend down at Covehead harbour with the newspaper with his picture in it sticking out of his pocket. Nobody's approached him yet.'

'Callendar did suggest his picture be in the paper,' Montagu said.

Croll nodded. 'So there you have it. Either the seal is in Callendar's safe, and he's sitting here acting worried, watching us fart around looking for it and laughing his head off. Or he's waiting for someone to contact him. I still like the first one best.'

'I don't,' Montagu said. 'Callendar is a perfectly respectable dealer. He gave us every guarantee against being cheated.'

'But not against the possibility that it would be stolen from your agent, from you, in effect. What happens now? Are you responsible?'

'It looks like it.' Suddenly Montagu threw a little tantrum. 'God almighty, Sergeant. As far as we know Callendar just fell over a good deal. Now you're suggesting he rigged up a plot to swindle us. The next thing you'll be saying he's behind the robbery of Clive's house. It's bizarre. I realize you have to be suspicious, but I'm glad I'm not a policeman.'

'Nobody's suggesting that,' Croll said.

A small chill settled over the three men. Croll looked at Salter, who said nothing for a few seconds. Then Salter said, slowly and carefully, 'Take offence if you like, Robert, but some of the politicians I've met make policemen look like church workers.'

Montagu flushed. 'I wasn't being personal.'

'Nor was I.'

Croll broke in. 'Callendar may not be a crook but he may be an opportunist. If I can convince a judge that the Marblehead dealer probably doesn't exist, then I can get a warrant to search his papers. But I'll be looking in the laundry basket for the seal. I'm going to start again with the correspondence from Elton.' He stood up.

Salter got to his feet quickly, embarrassed to be alone with his father-in-law after their little interchange. 'You're expected for dinner tomorrow, Robert,' he said.

Outside, Croll said, 'Touchy bastard, aren't you? Montagu

didn't mean anything by that crack about the police.'

'Sure he did. He just forgot I was there.'

Croll laughed. 'He'll be careful in future, won't he? Still, he's got a helluva nerve, You're right; with all due respect to your father-in-law, if he's going to go in for politics, he can forget about feeling superior to *anybody*.' Croll spoke without passion, delivering himself of a long-held opinion. The sentiment was banal, but the flatness in Croll's voice was extreme and Salter was provoked to inquire into it. 'You don't like politicians much?' he asked.

'I hate 'em,' Croll said cheerfully. 'The whole shooting match. Not because they lie and cheat and steal and give their pals fat jobs. Everybody does that. No, it's the way they make a fucking game out of my life. You ever been backstage at an election? When a bunch of them are talking politics and no one is listening? They don't give a shit about the country or you and me. Everything is turned into this game they have where they can outsmart the other side. Getting elected. The dollar goes up, the dollar goes down, fourteen per cent of the country are out of work, everything we eat is poisoned by radiation or pesticide, and the fish in Ontario are full of mercury. So what happens? Sweet fuck-all, because there are more votes and party donations that way. Isn't that right?'

'Probably,' Salter said. He was impressed by Croll's cheerful despair but retained for himself a romantic hope that somewhere in the system good men were still working for the common cause.

'Name one good, honest politician,' Croll said, mind-reading.

Salter did so.

'You may be right about him,' Croll conceded. 'Name another.'

Salter named another.

'He's dead. Name another.'

But Salter laughed and backed off. Croll, he realized,

had developed an anarchical disaffection for the process he served. Like a professional soldier, he concentrated on his skill at killing the enemy while the slogans of patriotism washed over his head in an obscene babble. Salter switched to another tack. 'Don't be too hard on Montagu,' he said. 'He's just an amateur.'

Croll looked as if he was considering letting Salter have Montagu. Then he shook his head. 'The ones who are just starting out—they're the worst. They get into the back room and hear the big boys figuring out how to manipulate us. A few of them get sick to their stomachs and quit, but the others think: Gee, is this the way it's done, and get sucked in right away. That's why it's the new boys who get caught. They see that it's done and they start in. Big expense trips all over the world, fat contracts for their pals. But they don't have the street-smarts of the old crooks and they get caught, so that even the journalists—who report this whole scene as if it's a game, by the way—have to notice. Then they get that stunned look on their faces when the referee throws them out of the game. Why me? they think. Everybody's doing it. Why am I the goat? Watch for the next landslide election, and then watch how many new ministers get caught in—what do they call it?—a conflict of interest. They're clumsy, see.'

'Feel better?' Salter asked.

Croll laughed. 'Montagu's all right, I guess. He's not a senator yet. But why did he blow up in there? He's not concerned about Elton. He's just pissed off that his little game might not work.'

'He can't do anything about Elton, but he might still be able to pull off this seal caper.'

'He could look *sorry*, couldn't he? *Sad*? But what's he really concerned about now? I'll tell you. He's worried that he may have been sucked in by Callendar in a way he never would've normally. He's a fine upstanding guy, your father-in-law, and a shrewd businessman, no doubt about it. But

now he might have made a horse's ass of himself over this
seal. Why? Because he got involved in politics and forgot
himself, lost his head, forgot his instincts. Aren't I right,
Charlie? Eh?'

Croll was probably right. Certainly, gullible or not, for
Montagu the death of Elton had been secondary to the loss
of the seal from the beginning, a point which Salter suspected
had troubled Annie. But mixed with his desire to defend his
in-law to Croll was Salter's totally reprehensible reaction
that he was glad that he didn't have to admire his father-in-
law quite so much in future. It would make the impact of
Annie's family on his world easier to resist.

That night Salter went to the races. For the visitor to Prince
Edward Island who wants to meet the Islanders on their
own ground, a visit to Charlottetown Raceway is essential.
Compared to the racing factories in Toronto and Montreal
it is a very modest operation: on a quiet night there may be
only a few hundred bettors, and a hundred dollars on a
horse will make a considerable difference to the odds.

The crowd is knowledgeable—everyone seems to know
someone who owns a trotter or a pacer—and since the same
horses race against each other frequently, major upsets are
rare. If the visitor backs the favourites all evening (not as
easy as it sounds because the wise or owner's money tends
to appear only at the last minute) he will not get hurt
much and he might make a small profit, enough to pay his
expenses. Salter had found it the pleasantest way to spend
an evening that the Island had to offer. He didn't go often,
because he liked to go alone, so he took the chance whenever
everyone else wanted to go to a movie that he didn't, for
example.

On this night, Annie wanted to spend some time with her
mother in Charlottetown, and Salter had the choice of
staying home with Sheila or finding something to do. He
chose the races. It was a fine evening, and he arrived at the

track in time to put five dollars on the first favourite which netted him a profit of two. He settled in to enjoy himself.

The crowd at the track is not only knowledgeable but familiar. They know each other, and even Salter had spent enough summers on the Island to run into someone occasionally he had met before, like the owner of the hardware store, or the mailman. It was no surprise, therefore, after the fourth race, when he was leaning over the rail watching the horses in the later races limbering up around the half-mile circuit, first to smell the candy-laden breath and then to hear the voice of Joe behind him.

'What are ye doin' on this one, Mr Salter?'

Salter turned around. He had plenty of time before the fifth and Joe might just have some information. 'Miss Muffet,' he said. 'What do you think?'

Joe looked at his card and chewed thoughtfully. He had changed his boots for a pair of Oxfords and put on a windbreaker, but the hat was still in place. 'Try Waltzing Sam,' he said. 'Fred Gallant owns him. I saw him put his money down already. He feels pretty sure of himself.'

Salter nodded, and the two men turned to watch the horses going round the track.

'How you gettin' on findin' that seal?' Joe asked.

'I'm not looking for it. The Mounties are.'

'That dealer fella any help yet?'

'Who do you mean?'

'The dealer fella. The one you came out fishin' with the other day.' Joe made an amused noise in his throat. 'He's been going round and round chatting to us all, asking if we know Mr Elton. Don't fool us, though. We seen what he's up to. He's wasting his time.'

'Why?'

'It's as plain as a boil on the end of your nose. The Mounties are using him for bait.'

'This is all news to me, Joe. How do you mean, bait?'

'We seen the other fella too. The Mountie, George

Dawson, follerin' him around. We all know George. It's a little trap the Mounties and the dealer fella have set up. The dealer's the bait, ye see, and George is on the other end of the line. Whatever that dealer's hopin', that someone would come forward, like, you talk to him, and George will reel you in. Plain as daylight. That's why they're wastin' their time.'

There was no reply to this. The local interpretation of events, however far off the mark, meant that Callendar was indeed wasting his time, and so was Croll. 'That's what you think is happening?' he asked.

'We all do. So if anyone knows anything about that seal they won't tell that dealer, will they?' He winked. 'You tell 'em, Mr Salter. And don't forget Waltzing Sam.' He strolled away towards the window.

I'll tell him, Salter thought. He followed Joe towards the window, noting the number of Waltzing Sam. Then, on grounds of superstition ('Never go off your first choice, Angus'), he put five dollars on Miss Muffet. In the event Waltzing Sam would have won easily but he broke stride and Miss Muffet got up to take it.

CHAPTER 10

The full story appeared the next day and Callendar left the Island on the afternoon plane. By then Fehely had done enough work on the ferry crossings to produce a list of names that had occurred repeatedly over the last year, a list of Islanders who regularly went back and forth, and of mainlanders who had visited the Island frequently. It took him two more days to eliminate all the salesmen, potato-wholesalers, lobster-vendors and others with mundane reasons for travelling back and forth, and to establish a pruned-down list of regular itinerants who were on the

Island on the night of Elton's death. When Salter called in to the station three days later, they had come up with a suspect.

'Diamond Jim,' Salter said. 'Holy Christ.'

'Who?' Croll asked.

'It's our family nickname for him. Diamond Jim Brady. Not just because of his name, but because he is kind of flashy, compared to the locals. An operator, a wheeler-dealer who hasn't made it yet. What about the robberies? Do they fit?'

'I've just finished checking those. He was on the Island for most if not all of them, as well as for the homicide. Do you know him?'

'Everyone around here knows him. He's into a lot of small things, but mostly he buys and sells furniture. Refinishes it. He's a good carpenter, too. A lot of people use him.'

'Ideal, then, isn't it? He must get to look inside a lot of houses. What's your impression of him?'

'A sharp character, but not as sharp as he thinks he is, or he wouldn't be buying and selling junk around here. He's the guy who offered to sell me some moonshine. Does he have a record?'

'We only just came up with his name. I've sent out a tracer.'

'Are you going to pick him up today?'

'As soon as I get everything I want. We'll wait for his record, if any. And I've sent his description to Toronto to see if they can identify him as the guy who was going round the dealers.'

'So what's the story? Brady has been robbing houses. Last week he got disturbed robbing Elton, killed him and ran. With the seal?'

'Maybe. But if Callendar *is* a rounder, he and Brady might have been in this from the start. Suppose Brady picked up the seal at an auction. He's one guy with just enough savvy to check it out. Suppose he checked it with

Callendar and they cooked up the deal. Then Callendar hands the seal over to Elton on Saturday, phones Brady that the deal is set and that the seal is on its way to the Island. Now, listen. Callendar doesn't have to be in on the next bit, but Brady might have seen an opportunity for himself. He could steal it back from Elton and he and Callendar would still get their money, and Brady could sell it again. But Elton came home and disturbed him.'

'You're off again, Brian. Did your man report any meeting between Brady and Callendar?'

'No, he didn't, but that may be Brady being smart.'

'Or it may be you are back to the other theory. That even if Brady and Callendar cooked up the original deal, when Elton was robbed it threw a monkey-wrench into the works. For a guy who's committed a homicide, he's acting very cool. I've seen him a couple of times since the homicide. I sat down and had a beer with him a few days ago, and he acted his old cocky self.'

'Okay, the robbery is probably a coincidence. I still don't trust Callendar not to be playing his own game. For all I know the seal is still in Toronto, or even Marblehead, though that's a shade less likely now. When you called me to tell me what Callendar had said, I did a little checking at the motel. Callendar never called Marblehead or even Toronto from his motel that day or the day before so he never spoke to any 'principal', not from his motel, anyway, and why would he go to the trouble of using a public call-box? I'm adding that to my request for a search warrant of Callendar's premises, by the way. It's still possible that someone entirely different, someone we don't know came across the seal and sold it to Callendar. I don't know. And with all due respect to your father-in-law, I don't give a fuck, either. I'm investigating a homicide, and Brady looks like a suspect. What would you do?'

'I'd pull him in. What else?'

But when Croll went to look for him, Brady was gone.

Croll asked Salter if he had any suggestions as to where Brady might be. 'He's still on the Island,' Croll said. 'At least we're pretty sure his truck hasn't gone out on the ferry. He doesn't have a record to speak of—one conviction for bringing skin magazines over the border into Ontario, but that was ten years ago. One dealer in Toronto thinks he's the one who offered him stuff. We went to get him this morning but he's disappeared.'

'I'll call you back.' Salter hung up and called Eleanor Vail.

'No,' she said. 'He was supposed to be here this morning to fix up some shelves. Who wants him?'

'The Mounties.'

'Oh dear. What has he done? Grown some pot in his back yard?'

'Something like that. Don't be surprised. You don't know him that well, do you?'

'Well enough. The idea wouldn't surprise me. What's the penalty for that on the Island. Ten years?'

Salter ignored this. 'If you do see or hear of him, let me or the police know, will you?'

'God Almighty,' she said, and hung up.

The search for Brady continued for two days. On the second day they found his truck parked in a quiet street in downtown Charlottetown, but they could find no one to swear how long it had been there. The Mountie at the airport could not remember Brady boarding a plane, either, but he *might* have, he agreed. It was the same story with foot passengers on ferries.

'He could have slipped out any time in the last three days,' Croll told Salter. 'By now he could be in Hong Kong. We've put the word out, of course, but three days is enough time for him to disappear. It isn't that hard.'

A search of Brady's house revealed nothing that could connect him with the robberies, or Elton's death, and there was no trace of the seal. In the meantime the search warrant on Callendar had also been executed, turning up no trace of any correspondence with a Marblehead principal, and no trace of the seal. Callendar's lawyer was now in the process of preparing a case against the RCMP for mounting a fishing expedition.

At home the news of Brady's disappearance caused more of a tremor than Salter expected. Sheila reacted with dismay and collapsed into silence, coming out of it after a few hours to announce she was leaving. 'I just don't feel like staying around,' she said. She refused to explain further, but later, to Annie, she revealed that she and Brady had become lovers while the Salters were in Halifax at the wedding.

'Jesus Christ,' Salter said, more in anger than in pity.

'It was so uncomplicated,' Annie reported. 'She told him at the auction you were all at on Friday that we were going to Halifax for the weekend, so he came by on Saturday to see if she was lonely. One thing led to another and he stayed the night. Don't say anything to her.'

'Like what?' Salter was irritated. 'But might he have told her anything about himself that would help Croll?'

'I'll ask her, but if she says not, can we keep her out of it? She's very upset.'

'She hardly knew the guy. Why should it hit her so hard?'

'Don't be stupid. Of course she's upset. She was making love with a killer, maybe.'

'Okay. Explain to her that the police will want to find out everywhere he's been lately, including the auction. Tell her that if she can remember anything he told her about who he knew around the Island, who he dealt with, anything, it might help.'

Annie went into Sheila's room and the two women came out together after a few minutes. Sheila was looking miserable, but she spoke to Salter calmly. 'You know about me

and Jim, don't you? Annie said she'd told you.' She wiped
her nose with a tissue. 'So that's it. All we talked about
was furniture. He explained what he looked for to sell in
Toronto.'

'I'll tell Croll you went to the auction with him, that's
all. And that you don't know anything else about him.'

'It's true. Nothing.'

'Okay. Annie said you wanted to leave this afternoon.
When you're ready I'll take you in.'

Salter drove her to the airport, pondering his duty. Like
Annie, he was now inclined to feel sorry for his house-guest.
He decided that her small encounter with Brady was no
business of Croll's.

It wasn't until Brady's body surfaced, literally, three days
later, that Salter told Croll her story. One of the in-shore
fishermen working out of Tignish netted the body when he
was dragging for ground-fish. Around Brady's waist were
the marks of a cable or rope. The back of his head had been
sheared away by a shotgun blast, some pellets from which
still lodged in his skull.

Brady's death brought home to Angus the reality of his
father's work. Policemen do not usually take their work
home with them so that it remains an abstraction to their
children, but Brady was someone Angus had met, and Salter
found the boy wanting to know for the first time about the
world of killers, victims and cops. The final effect was to
enlarge Angus's new admiration for his father. Annie was
appalled. Brady had no charms for her, but she had been
entertained by his swashbuckling manner and its effect on
Sheila. Her comment was, 'Will the Toronto papers pick it
up?' Thereafter she avoided the subject.

Salter's reaction was to feel sorry for Croll, who was now
looking for another killer before he could be sure he had
found the first one. Croll must assume the two deaths were
related and search among Brady's connections for a cause.
He decided it was not the time to suggest otherwise. Later,

perhaps. But after another chat with the lava man he changed his mind.

When Tom Gush's truck pulled up by the back door the next morning, Salter waylaid him. 'Like some coffee?' he asked. 'Come on up to the house and have a cup.'

Gush climbed out of the truck. 'Right you are. You bring it out here. I'm not very tidy.'

Salter collected two cups of coffee from Annie and returned to the truck. 'You heard the police found Brady?' he asked. 'What do you think happened to him?'

'I wouldn't know anything about Brady,' Gush said. 'We were never pals, I told you.' He closed the door of his truck and stood still, attentive. 'But I think I may have been a bit responsible for some of them robberies he did.'

'You think he was the thief?'

'It's all over the Island. Police have been questioning everybody who was robbed to find out if Brady was working nearby at the time. I know for a fact he was working on some of them. And I believe I may have helped him, unbeknownst to me.'

'How?'

'We used to stop and exchange the time of day sometimes. He often used to ask me when I knew people was away. He seemed to want to know about everybody, where they was and how long they were away for. I reckon he went round gossiping all over, picking up the news. I see now what he was up to.' Gush nodded savagely to himself.

'Who else did he talk to?'

'Brady knew everybody, I reckon. If he kept his ears open in the Legion hall he'd hear enough to keep him busy. I've seen him several times at tables, talking to people like meself —drivers, deliverymen and such.' He leaned against the door of his truck and crossed his arms. 'He knew more about some of my customers than I did—where they come from, how they made their money, that sort of thing. He was like a damn barber for gossip.'

'So what do you think happened?'

'We all reckon it was on account of his chasing tail too much. Someone caught him bare-arsed, we think, and laid for him.'

'You don't think someone might have killed him to get hold of this seal they're talking about?'

Gush made a loud, explosive noise of disgust, a 'pah' of contempt. 'We don't reckon nothing to that story. I don't believe there ever was a seal. Answer me this. If there was a seal why hasn't it turned up before this? Mr Elton never mentioned it and he used to chat to me quite a bit. Somebody said they talked to his cleaning lady and she'd never heard of it. I think the Mounties made that one up.'

'Why?'

'You can't tell with them fellas. If there was a seal then someone lost it before all this, and the Mounties couldn't find it, and now they're using this as a cover-up. That's what we think. That dealer fella, maybe,' he ended mysteriously.

Salter was impressed at how thoroughly the case had been discussed in the Legion halls. 'So why was Elton killed?' he asked.

'Because he disturbed the fella who was robbin' him. And you know who that was.'

'Brady?'

'Who else?' Gush climbed up into his truck.

'You think they'll ever find out who killed Brady?' Salter asked.

'All they've got to do is find out who caught Brady diddling his wife. That's all.'

'So the way I see it,' he said later to Croll, 'is that he probably jumped on any woman who looked likely. He's like the guy in the joke—he gets his face slapped a lot, but he got laid a lot, too. Brady got around. He wasn't married—'

'Yes, he was. He had a wife and four children in Guelph,

Ontario. She hadn't seen him for two years.'

'Is that right?' Salter smiled. 'He was behind on his support payments, was he?'

'How the hell would I know? She doesn't want any part of him, she says. But she's claiming anything he owned.'

'I just wondered. But he had no regular woman on the Island, and he sure as hell liked women. This guy who delivers our chickens knew him a bit and said that Brady had a name for screwing around.'

'What are you telling me?'

'Maybe you've just got an Island husband or boyfriend who has found out that Brady has been jumping his wife or girl, or daughter. So he finds out where they meet and he waits for him with a shotgun.'

'It's a possibility. So we have to scratch around trying to locate any girlfriend of Brady's with a jealous guy in the background.'

'Have you talked to Brady's neighbours yet?'

'Oh yes. They saw him take your visitor home the other day, after the auction. She was there about an hour. You're probably right that she can't tell us anything.'

'Do the neighbours report anyone else going in or out?'

'No, but that makes sense, doesn't it? None of the local ladies would want to risk being seen, and they sure as hell would have been. But your visitor didn't have to care about local gossip, did she? No, if Brady was screwing around he'd have found other places to go. What I'm hoping, though, is that there is a connection between Elton's death and Brady. Otherwise we've got the usual goddamn job of going round the three counties door-to-door with Brady's picture, asking anyone if they've seen him lately. As far as I'm concerned, Brady killed Elton, and I want the guy who killed him. Brady fits all right. At one time or another he had worked on a lot of the houses that were robbed, and from what you say, he kept his ear to the ground about the comings and goings of the Islanders.'

'Where will you start?'

'Here's what I've got.' Croll turned a map of the Island at an angle so that Salter could see it. 'The truck was parked in Charlottetown, and Brady's body surfaced here.' He pointed to a spot slightly east of Miminegash. 'Brady had been dead for three days and the body might have worked loose any time after he was put into the sea. He was still on the bottom, though, because they found him when they were dragging for ground-fish. The fishermen told me they thought it was another horse.'

'A what?'

'A couple of years ago someone went harvesting Irish moss. You know how they do that? They take a horse out as far as it can walk with a big rake attached. This time they went too far out and the horse bolted and tried to swim to New Brunswick. They brought it up in their net ten days later. So the fishermen who found Brady's body thought they had another horse. Anyway, the fisheries people tell me that the tide or current or whatever would have shifted the body east, towards Charlottetown. They figure the body was dumped not far from where it was found, but west of it, if anything.'

'From a boat?'

'It had to be. He was in deep enough water.'

A remark of Tom Gush's from an earlier conversation came back to Salter. 'Brady got into a fight with someone once, some fisherman from Summerside who caught him with his wife.'

'Did he, by Christ? Who was that?'

'Ask Gush. He told me.'

'I'll do that. So I think we are looking for a man with a boat and that's why we are questioning all the fishermen on the South Shore first. By the time we're through, we'll have questioned just about everybody on the Island, all because of some sleazy bastard from away.'

'You sound like an Islander.'

Croll turned from Salter and looked out the window. 'I feel like one. I love this place. I've been here eight years— my longest stay in one place since I was twenty—and like I told you, if they try and shift me I'll resign—I'm qualified for a pension. This is the first place that's felt like home, you know? My neighbours have accepted me, and you know how hard that is for a cop anywhere. It's where my kids have spent their growing years, and my wife loves it.'

'It's a peaceful place,' Salter said, wondering privately what people did here from September to June.

'That's right. It is. Peaceful. We had a big drug bust this spring—two pounds of marijuana. There are lawyers in Toronto with that much in the freezer. Apart from that, our big problem is drunken driving. It's got something to do with the fact that it's an island. For a cop my age, it's a nice place to be.' Croll leaned towards Salter and continued speaking urgently, as if Salter was disagreeing with him. 'It's a working man's province, Charlie. I can afford to do anything I want on this Island. Where else could I go fly-fishing for five dollars a year? And catch fish. Where else could I join the Yacht Club?'

'You belong to the Yacht Club?'

'No, but I *could*. And come and see my house sometime, then tell me what I'd have to pay in Toronto for the same thing. I've got the *beach* at the end of my garden.' Croll subsided back into his chair. 'It makes me feel protective,' he ended.

Then he began again. 'You ever looked at the Island on a map of Canada, Charlie? You know these assholes who brag to Americans that this is the second biggest country in the world? Sure it is, but most of it is uninhabitable, for Chrissake. You ever been north? The Arctic? I have. I spent six years up there, most of it in the Yukon. When I got the posting I was pretty excited. You know, you read these stories as a kid about the Royal North West Mounted Police, how they captured Trapper Johnson and stuff. That's why

I joined in the first place. I thought the Yukon was blue skies, two feet of snow and me, on horseback, bringing the law to the natives. It's not like that. There are three seasons up there, the blackfly season, the mosquito season, and winter. They talk about dry cold as if it doesn't hurt, but dry, wet, forty below is a killer. I hated it. So where else? Saskatchewan and Manitoba can get pretty bleak in the winter, except in the cities. So there's the Maritimes. New Brunswick was better than the north, but this place is the best. It's ridiculous to have a province this small in a country this big, but it's *nice*. And I want to keep it that way.' Croll subsided again. 'Now let's get back to work.'

'I've heard people swear the North is the only place to live.'

'So have I. I've met them, too, and they aren't faking it. Good luck to them. They can have it. I've been there.'

CHAPTER 11

Croll covered every possibility. His men questioned everyone along the South Shore, all the bartenders and waiters in every likely Legion hall; they talked to everyone who had had dealings with Brady, everyone who had sold anything to him or had work done by him. They questioned the people who had been robbed, but while three of them had actually employed Brady in the last year, most had never met him. They looked for anyone who had a grudge against Brady, someone he might have swindled, and, as far as rumours would lead them, any husbands or boyfriends who might have caught Brady with their women. But since he bought mostly at auctions, they could find no one aware of having been cheated. In the other area of Brady's interests, they found one widow in Alberton whom Brady had been known to visit—the neighbours were fully aware of it—but there was no one in the shadows behind her defending her honour with a shotgun. Not, she shouted, that there was anything for her to be ashamed of. Brady had done one or two little jobs around the house for which she had paid in cash, so who was the dirty-minded cow who was trying to blacken her name?

With Tom Gush's help they found the fisherman who had beaten up Brady. He was pleased that Brady was dead because he probably had it coming to him, but the man gave a solid account of himself for the past week, and they were obliged to release him. They found no other fisherman along the South Shore with the slightest link to Brady's amorous or professional activities. No one had even heard of him until his death. But the discovery of Brady's body created another development.

On the Palmer Road, which joins the road to Miminegash near St Louis, a farmhouse had been broken into while the owner was away. The owner was a Toronto professor who had bought the farm the summer before, planning to use it for his family vacations. When he arrived to take up residence he found that in his absence the place had been torn apart—cupboards emptied, mattresses thrown around, and even floorboards ripped up. He had left nothing valuable in the house, which had perhaps irritated the robbers into what looked like pure vandalism. The owner had gone in search of the man he had been paying to look after his farm during the winter, and finding him not at home, had come to the police, for the caretaker was Jim Brady. He had done some work on the farmhouse the previous summer and offered for a fee to keep an eye on the place during the winter, an offer which the owner, fearing just the kind of vandalism that had occurred, had gladly accepted.

When the police investigated they could find no one among the neighbours who had noticed anything wrong, except for the state of the property. Brady had done nothing to earn his fee, probably planning a massive clean-up the day before the owner arrived, and the neighbours were cool towards the misfortunes of the man from away who was using one of their farms as a summer cottage. It was easy to share their indifference: the grass in the yard was waist high, the gate sagged open on one sound hinge and the steps on to the front porch had broken off and fallen forward. In the nearby town of St Louis, a descendant of the original settler who had cleared the land was still living, an old man himself, watching his heritage turn into a rotting playhouse.

The owner could find nothing that had been stolen, but the search revealed a further indignity in the shape of some used condoms in the main bedroom, suggesting that the farm had been a regular trysting-place. Although the usual beer bottles were not around, it seemed possible that one couple, or group of couples, old enough to use the place as a love-nest were also young enough or hooligan enough to trash the place when the party was over. It was hardly worthwhile, in view of the slight material damage, mounting another major investigation, but Croll could not overlook anything which might lead him to Brady and promised to make inquiries.

The police scoured the area around St Louis, looking for anyone who might have used the main bedroom, and by hard questioning and sifting malicious gossip, which in turn generated counter-accusations, they netted three men who admitted to having enjoyed the farm's facilities, which led to the general admission that it was a place where everyone went if he had a girl who was willing. There was even a code. No one was foolish enough to park a car or truck in the yard, or in the Palmer Road, because even the most indifferent neighbour might then have called the police. But behind the farm there was a lane that connected to a road to the beach, and it was understood that if you found a vehicle parked in the lane, then someone was there before you and you looked for somewhere else.

Croll interviewed the three men one by one, frightening

them a little, then asking for their cooperation. 'You've been breaking and entering,' he told them. 'But I don't care about that. What I want to find out is when the place was trashed.'

One of them identified the possible day that he and his girl had arrived and found the place in a mess and got out immediately for fear of being caught and blamed for the damage. Another man who had no idea of what Croll was talking about admitted using the house several days before, but had seen nothing wrong, so Croll was able to pinpoint the damage to the day before they had set out to arrest Brady. Croll's men went from house to house once more, searching for anyone who had sighted Brady's truck in the area, or any other truck or car parked near the farm, but here the investigation dried up. A few over-eager 'maybe's', unreliable and probably false, was the best they could do. The neighbours now admitted that they had their suspicions that someone was using the place from time to time, but since they guessed it was only kids, they ignored them. Let the guy who owned the place worry. The Toronto fella.

In the course of the questioning the police ran across a fisherman in Miminegash who complained that someone had borrowed his dory the week before, taken it from the part of the beach where he always left it and returned it a hundred yards down the beach. The owner's real complaint was that whoever borrowed the boat had stolen the anchor and about fifty yards of new rope he had just bought.

It was the Toronto owner of the farmhouse who telephoned to say that one of his children, playing in an outbuilding, had uncovered a pile of jewellery.

Croll called Salter. 'I told him not to touch it. We'd be there in an hour and a half. It looks as if we might have the seal. Wanna come and claim it?'

'You think it will be there?'

'Seems likely. I'm in Charlottetown now and I'm going to leave in about fifteen minutes. Hang on, let me look at the map. Here. If you want to come, meet me in Miscouche.

There's a big white church at the crossroads. I'll look for
you there, but if I don't see you I won't wait.' He hung up.

Angus was on the porch, throwing darts at a board. 'Come
for a ride,' Salter said. 'Drive me up to Miscouche and then
bring the car back.'

Angus, still eager to get behind a wheel at any opportunity, grabbed his sneakers and mashed his feet into them.
'What's up, Dad?'

'I'm going up to the other end of the Island with the
Mounties. Hurry up; they're not going to wait.'

On the way, Salter told Angus of the latest development.
They reached Miscouche before Croll, and Salter and Angus
got out of the car to wait. Croll appeared almost immediately. Salter introduced Angus to him and moved to climb
into the Mountie's car while Angus waited to see them go,
yearning palpably.

Croll said, 'Want to come along, young fella?'

Salter shrugged when Angus looked at him questioningly,
and the boy leaped into the back seat.

'Lock our car first,' Salter said.

Angus jumped out and rushed around their car, fumbling
with the keys, still on the edge of the world where adults
change their minds for no good reason.

When he had regained the Mountie's car, Croll said, 'If
it comes to a take-down, young fella, you go in first and
your dad and I will cover you. I've got the guns in the
trunk.'

Salter said, 'You will stay right out of the way. All right?'

The road to Tignish took them through a part of the
Island much less visited by tourists than the Cavendish
area. From the air the province is a single bright green
crescent with a dark ochreous fringe along the South Shore
where the sands bleed into the sea, but the three counties
into which the Island is divided look very different from the
highway. The centre of the Island, Queens County, is Green
Gables' land, a neatly pretty, rolling landscape of small

farms and picturesque villages with, along the north shore, the immaculately manicured National Park, a lovely playground which is deserted most of the year. Tourist country. Now they were driving through Prince County, towards the Acadian end of the Island; long stretches of the highway wound through dreary scrub, land wiped clean of its original timber by lumber entrepreneurs and never restored. The villages were simply groups of houses and gas stations, huddled together at the crossroads. As they moved further west, more and more of the houses looked in need of repair and even some of the gas stations looked derelict, though they were all functioning as far as Salter could tell.

When he commented on it, Croll said, 'It's a pity. This end of the Island is a hell of a lot more real than Cavendish Beach. Where we are going has some of the best beaches on the Island, and even in August you won't find many people on them. The thing is, tourists with kids have trouble finding what they need at this end of the Island, hamburgers and ice-cream and stuff, so they feel deprived and go back to Cavendish. So you can't make a concession pay for those who do come. It's a vicious circle. It's changing a little bit.' He pointed to a Kentucky Fried Chicken outlet on the highway. 'The purists complain about that, but it's a hell of a welcome sight to a man with a car full of tired, hungry kids on a rainy day. And it can rain here, all right. But this end is a paradise for real campers.'

They turned off at a sign for St Louis, continued for a mile, then turned off again, coming to the Palmer Road church.

'Big, isn't it?' Croll said. 'It serves a big area.'

'Are they all French Catholic around here?'

'Most of them. Descendants of the ones who hid out when the English tried to deport all the French in the eighteenth century.'

'Why haven't I heard of an Acadian Society, like you have in New Brunswick?'

'There *is* a society. It just isn't very big or vocal. Only fifteen per cent of the population is French, and they are mostly farmers and fishermen. In the past, the odd French kid who got through high school tended to wind up somewhere else, in Montreal, taking a law degree or some such, and he stayed there when he graduated. It's changing a bit as the standards of education go up across the country, but the population has stayed about the same for the last fifty years. Stable, they call it, and it doesn't make for many changes. You might call it stagnant, but it's got a lot going for it. There's a huge culture lag, as they say, between us and the rest of Canada, but it does give you a chance to see what's going wrong on the mainland and stop it crossing on the ferry.'

The car slowed as they came to the end of the paved road, and they bumped along rutted gravel for another mile.

'What happened?' Angus asked from the back seat.

'It's a classic case. One of the farmers told me. They are all Liberal around here and it's taken six elections to get the road this far. About a mile an election. They reckon there'll be three or four more before the road gets to the highway. Here we are.' Croll slowed and stopped by a farm gate. The two policemen got out. 'Come on, Angus,' Croll said, and the boy scurried to join them.

Two men in early middle age were attempting to scythe the grass that grew waist deep in the yard. They were working side by side and had been at it long enough to look exhausted by the unnatural exercise. One of them, a thin, fair-haired man whose pale skin was reddening across the shoulders, put down his scythe as the car pulled up and walked to the gate. Three young children pelted out of the barn and ran to form a ring around him.

'Mr Curnow?' Croll asked.

The man nodded and opened the gate for them. 'For this relief, much thanks,' he said.

'Where is it?'

'I'll show you. Clarissa found it. Perhaps she should lead the way.'

A round-faced girl about five years old immediately went scarlet and buried her face in Curnow's legs.

'Don't you want to show the policeman?' Curnow asked.

For answer, the girl burrowed deeper into the back of his knees.

'I'll show them,' a chunky boy of about six said. 'I know where they are.'

The other boy, dark-haired and thin, but obviously the chunky boy's brother, threw himself on the ground and started to scream. 'I wanted to show them,' he howled.

'I'm showing them,' the chunky boy said.

The yells of the dark-haired boy increased. From across the yard, the other man called, 'Thomas, stop it. Harold spoke first. Get up.'

From somewhere inside himself the dark boy found a way of increasing the volume. The man put down his scythe and walked over to where the boy lay. 'Stop it,' he said, and nudged the boy lightly with his knee. For answer the boy rolled over and sank his teeth in his father's ankle.

'God Almighty,' the man said, and grabbed the boy by the neck and hit him on the bottom seven or eight times. A woman appeared from the house shaking her head and muttering, 'For heaven's sake,' picked up the boy who was now writhing in affected pain and real frustration, and carried him by an arm and leg into the house.

The boy's father took out a short curly pipe and lit it. 'Never hit a child except in anger,' he said to the policemen, and went back to his scything.

Salter looked at Angus. 'Advice,' he said. 'Make a note of it.'

'I think we can go now,' Curnow said. 'Lead the way, Harold.' They formed up into a procession behind the boy who took them around the barn to a long low building beyond, the original chicken house. Inside, Harold marched over to one of a row of nesting boxes and pointed, just as Clarissa, fighting off her shyness, raced to get in front of him and shouted, 'It's in here,' before she ran back behind her father.

They were lying uncovered in the box, a small pile of rings and other jewellery, as well as some pieces of silver. In with them was a gunny sack.

'Is this how you found them?' Croll asked.

The girl put her head round her father's knees. 'No,' she shouted, 'they were in that bag.'

Salter picked up the gunny sack and jerked back sharply. Croll laughed. 'You ever been on a chicken farm? It's just about the worst stink you can get.'

Gingerly Salter held the bag by the corners and shook it upside down. A gold ring fell out. Croll took a pencil out of his pocket and turned the jewellery over, separating and spreading it out. 'This all of it?' he asked Curnow.

'Did you take any away, Clarissa?' Curnow asked.

'No. Harold did.'

'I didn't,' Harold shouted back. 'Just to show you.'

'Harold brought a ring out to where we were working,' Curnow said. 'I don't think anything is missing. I called you right away and the children were forbidden to touch after that.'

'Not there?' Salter asked, not wanting to look himself.

Croll shook his head. 'You sure nothing is missing?' he asked Curnow and the two children.

'No one took anything,' Harold said. 'I stood guard.'

'And you found it all in the sack?' Croll asked the girl, who nodded, moving her head through a single giant arc.

The two policemen checked the other nesting boxes and the rest of the building, then Croll got a plastic bag from his car and deposited the stuff in it, piece by piece, using a Kleenex to handle it. Salter held the gunny sack questioningly and Croll shrugged. 'Sure,' he said. 'Let the lab people have the full experience.' Salter dropped the sack into the plastic bag.

'Thank you,' Croll said to Curnow. 'We've been looking for this stuff. Thank you, too, Clarissa,' he added. Clarissa went scarlet and disappeared behind her father again.

In the car, Croll said, 'Curnow's a professor from Toronto. So is his pal, I would think.'

'I didn't think they were farmers.'

Croll smiled. 'That settles it for the robberies, I guess. This is where Brady kept the stuff. But there's no goddamn seal, so tough titty for old Montagu.'

'You'll give the farm a proper search?'

'Just in case he kept it in a special place? Sure.' Croll sighed. 'Whoever trashed the place might have been looking for the seal, too, you know that?'

'Could be. But it's the same kind of mess that punks would make, so I wouldn't build on it.'

'I'm not *certain*, Salter, but it's *likely*, isn't it, for Chrissake? It's a good bet, too, that Brady found the mess and knew who it was and got killed looking for him.'

'Oh, sure,' Salter said placatingly.

'Then *that*'s the tack I'm going to take. In the meantime, I've found Elton's killer, haven't I? So there's one down and one to go. Right? All I have to do now is find the guy who killed Brady.'

'And the seal,' Salter said incautiously.

'I want to meet someone who's seen it, apart from Callendar, before I worry too much about that,' Croll said, and Salter knew he was solving the problem by refusing to believe it existed, which he was entitled to do.

The disappointment at not finding the seal had created a sense of let-down in the car, and when Croll suggested they go back by a different route Salter agreed, sharing his desire to get something out of the afternoon. Croll turned back to St Louis and from there drove up to Miminegash Pond and along Lady Slipper Drive, following the coast road past the superb, nearly empty beaches towards West Cape, inviting them to compare this part of the coast with the honky-tonk world of Cavendish. At West Cape he turned inland to O'Leary, pointing out a couple of good fishing spots along the way.

'Is fly-fishing tricky?' Salter asked.

'You want to come?'

'I don't have the gear.'

'I'll lend you some. When this case is over, I'll give you a lesson. I'll take you over to the Bonshaw River. The tourists pass it on their way to all the other spots. It's a bit late in the season, but we should raise some. Are you on?'

'Sure. I'd like that.'

'How about you, young fella?'

'No, thanks. I hate fresh-water fishing.'

Croll laughed. 'Here's the church,' he said. He pulled up beside Salter's car. 'I won't forget.'

CHAPTER 12

Croll's assumption came to pieces very quickly. At dinner with Eleanor Vail that Saturday night, the talk moved immediately on to the only Island topic of any interest. Sheila's early departure was explained as boredom, the real reason put into the back of the closet.

'She was a bit upset, too,' Annie said. 'She'd enjoyed the auction with Brady, and I think she was hoping he might take her again. It was the most interesting thing that had happened to her here.'

'He was?' Eleanor asked.

'*It* was. Going to a farm auction.'

Eleanor did not put much energy into the discussion of Brady's death, only joining in when Salter told the story of the robberies that were now laid at Brady's door.

'Do the police think he killed Elton?' she asked.

Here Salter closed down. So far he had been disseminating public knowledge, or knowledge that would soon be public. But the police assumption of a connection between Brady and Elton was not his to share. He compromised by pointing out the obvious. 'If Brady was the robber, which looks certain, and if he was robbing Elton that night, then the odds on his killing Elton look pretty good, don't they?'

'How will they establish that?'

'I don't know. They'll turn Brady's place upside down for a weapon. They've done that. If they find anything the forensic people can identify, then that will be that. And they'll go the other route. They'll have the technicians go over Elton's house and body for some trace of Brady.'

'What if they don't find anything?'

'They will also try to check on Brady's movements that night. He often spent Saturday night in the club here in Marlow, and Elton was killed after the club was closed. Brady wasn't under suspicion before. Now they'll look for someone, anyone, who might have been with him that night. Maybe even a partner in the robberies.'

'And if Jim is unaccounted for, they'll assume he was involved?'

'They'll assume it's likely. They've been trying to find a pattern from the beginning, someone who knows when people are away and someone who is selling the loot. Brady fits both categories. He got around, fixing things the way he did for you, and kept his ears open for news of people going out of town.'

'I see. Just a minute. I'll get the dessert.' She stood up and started to collect plates.

'I'll do it, Eleanor,' Angus said, jumping up. He was still deeply in love with her, a condition she handled with tact while she waited for him to turn her back into a frog. But this time she only shook her head. 'I'll manage,' she said firmly, and disappeared into the kitchen. 'Pour some more wine, will you, Charlie,' she called from inside the kitchen. 'I'll just be a few minutes. Maybe you could find us another record, Angus.'

They waited for more than fifteen minutes before she re-emerged, bearing a piece of cheese and some crackers. 'I forgot to buy coffee,' she said. 'Can I borrow some from you, Annie?'

Annie started to get up.

'Angus could fetch it,' Eleanor said. 'Would you mind, Angus?'

He was gone, and when the door closed behind him, Eleanor said, 'I need some advice. What difference would it make to the police to know that Jim couldn't possibly have killed Elton?'

'Quite a bit. They'd have to start looking for another robber. They'd have three separate crimes, not necessarily connected: a lot of robberies, a homicide, and another homicide.'

'And if they worked on the assumption that Jim was the robber who killed Elton, then they would forget about looking for Elton's killer, and just look for someone who had it in for Jim, and whoever killed Elton would get away with it?'

'Possibly.'

Eleanor joined her hands in front of her. 'Right, then. Before Angus gets back, Jim was with me when Elton died.'

Annie folded her napkin and looked at Salter.

'What time?' Salter asked.

Annie got up and began clearing the detritus of the main course. Eleanor looked at her briefly, then continued. 'We had dinner, and then he had breakfast.'

'He was your lover?'

'For God's sake, Charlie. Angus will be back in a minute,' Annie said. 'What's Eleanor to do?'

'Tell Croll, of course.' There was the sound of Angus

walking up on to the porch. 'I'll go with you.'

'Does it become public then?'

'No. It's nobody's business. Nobody else's, I mean. I'll come for you about nine in the morning.'

Angus walked in bearing the coffee. 'What's nobody's business?' he asked.

'That's for us to know and you to find out,' Annie said, breaking all the rules. 'Go and grind the coffee.'

'I think it's about Mr Brady and Sheila,' Angus said.

'*Go and grind the coffee*,' Annie repeated.

He disappeared into the kitchen.

'What's he talking about?' Eleanor asked. 'Oh, I see.'

'That's nobody's business, too,' Annie declared.

'Well, well,' Eleanor said, looking at her folded hands. 'Our Jim got around, didn't he?' She got up and took a bottle of brandy from the cupboard, and put it on the table with some glasses. 'Well, well,' she said again. 'I feel a bit of a bloody fool, but only because you're here. What about Sheila? Was she very upset?'

'Yes, she was,' Annie said.

'She'd be even more upset if she were here, so let's keep it all in the family,' Salter suggested.

Angus returned. 'All done,' he reported. 'But I don't know how to make espresso.'

'I'll do it. Thanks, Angus.'

When Eleanor had gone, Angus looked craftily around the table. 'She had coffee all the time,' he mouthed in a whisper. 'I saw it in the cupboard. She just wanted to get me out of the way. What were you talking about?'

'Sex,' Salter said promptly. 'Okay?'

Angus grinned. 'I think you were talking about food. That's all you people ever talk about.'

When Salter led Eleanor into Croll's office in Charlottetown the next morning, Croll said, 'I was just going to call you.' He looked at Eleanor. 'What's up?'

Salter introduced her to Croll and she told her story. Croll listened and said nothing. When she had finished, there was a long silence, and Salter stood up.

Now Croll spoke. 'Hold on, Charlie, I've got some news for you, too. Thank you, Miss Vail.' He nodded to dismiss her. Salter said, 'She has to get back to Marlow. Will we be long?'

For answer, Croll pressed a buzzer and ordered the constable who appeared to take Eleanor home.

'Well, well, well,' Croll said, when she was gone. 'We can rely on her, can we?'

'Yes. It took some nerve for her to tell us.'

'She's not keeping his memory sacred, or any bullshit like that, is she?'

'She's not a kid. She spent fifteen minutes in the kitchen making up her mind to tell us. She'd have realized how silly she would look if you could prove that Brady wasn't with her. He was with her all right.'

'So we need a new killer. Any ideas?' Croll said, sourly.

'You are going to have to keep asking until someone remembers who was driving around the night Elton got killed.'

'And Brady?'

'Find out where he was killed.'

'I have.' And then Croll told Salter about the two men he had sent to search the farm just in case Clarissa was lying. They did not find the seal, but on the door of the barn they found a smeared, pock-marked area which turned out to be a patch of dried blood dotted with shotgun pellets. 'So Brady was shot in the barn. Then he was dumped in the drink. Why?'

'He caught someone trashing the place?'

'That's what I think, too. The regular robber never made that kind of mess. Now, if Brady was the robber, what was he doing getting killed in the barn by some other guy?'

'It's where he kept the loot. You never found anything in Brady's house, did you?'

'So someone might have known he kept the stuff there and come looking for it. Brady interrupted him and got killed, the way Elton interrupted *his* killer.'

'Not the seal?'

'I don't need a seal. I've got a robber—Brady—and I'm looking for someone who knew he kept the stuff at the farmhouse and decided to steal it off him. Fuck the seal.'

The area around Palmer Road was combed repeatedly for anyone who had heard a shotgun blast, but the sound of a shotgun inside the barn is no more than a loud thud a hundred yards away, and no one had heard anything. Once more the area where they had found Brady's truck was sifted, because, reasoned Croll, whoever shot Brady drove his truck to the airport and left. He also might now be in Hong Kong.

'Unless,' Salter said, 'that's what he wants you to think.'

But Croll followed the sensible course of investigating the obvious, and checked again on every known foot passenger who had left the Island by air or ferry, and his men inquired after anyone who had been missing since Brady's death. With no results.

'I'm meeting my father-in-law in the morning,' Salter said, the next day. 'Can I give him any message about the seal?'

'Sure. Tell him he can probably forget about it, seeing it again. If he feels honour bound to pay Callendar, he should go ahead. I wouldn't myself, but like he said, I'm naturally suspicious.'

'Why?'

'Because the longer we go without it, the more I think it isn't on the Island, and that it never was on the Island, and that it has nothing to do with these guys getting killed. You know that no one said a word about it, not Elton to his girlfriend, not Brady to any of his women, and no one has laid eyes on it. I think Elton never brought it back. I think Callendar got to his safe before we did.' All this was delivered in something close to a shout.

When Salter reported this to Montagu, later that morning, Montagu agreed.

'If that's the case then I'll wait a bit,' he said. 'But if they don't find it I'll have to pay up. At least we will have established ownership rights to the thing. If it ever does surface, we can claim it.'

'It hasn't done your party much good, has it?'

'No harm though. The Opposition has tried to make a case for the Premier being irresponsible, but they're making a balls-up of it and it's backfiring on them. The fact is, it wouldn't have been worth much in the way of votes. Seventeen per cent of the Island is unemployed, and their attitude is, frankly, bugger the seal, find me a job. There's a letter in the paper today to that effect. The attendant over in the museum reports a few more tourists asking about it, but the locals don't care much. Still, you know, it wasn't all politics. Some of us were really interested in getting the seal back. It was exciting for a while.'

'Oh, sure. Well, I must be off. Annie and I are finally on our own now that Sheila's gone. How is Seth, by the way?'

'He's fine. His grandmother is feeling guilty about having him with us all the time, but she enjoys him, so do his uncles, and the boy likes sailing so much . . .'

'Don't sweat. Let the kid have the holiday he came for.'

'How is Angus enjoying himself?'

'He's left us, too. I dropped him off at the club this morning. He wanted to go out with Seth, so you might have both of them staying with you tonight.'

'Why don't we keep the pair of them for a couple of days? Then you and Annie could have a bit of a rest yourselves. If you want.'

'Okay. Tell him not to come home, then. He can call us tomorrow.'

Salter left Montagu's office with some time to spare before he was due home for lunch and he walked over to the Confederation Centre to talk to the museum officials. They listened to him and directed him to the archives office where he was shown a picture of the seal, mounted on a display board.

'That's not the seal, of course,' the official in charge said. 'It's said to be a wax impression of the original. There's no proof of that, either.'

'You mean it might not be a real picture?'

'Obviously it's a real picture, but there is some doubt whether the wax replica is authentic.'

Salter thought about this and decided that what he was hearing was just professional caution. 'Could I take a picture of this?' he asked.

'No, but I can let you have a copy.'

'When?'

'Right now. I made several from the negative. I've already had a request from the RCMP.'

Have you, indeed, Salter thought. Ah well. 'I'd like one, too, please. Is there a charge?'

'Four dollars.' The official produced the picture and took Salter's money.

'Where is this wax replica?' Salter asked. 'Did the Mounties take it?'

'No. We never had it. I don't think they asked. I've never seen it myself, but according to Lorne Callbeck's book it's in the possession of the Historical Society.'

'Where's that?'

'It's the last building on Kent Street.'

But the Historical Society was unable to produce the replica either. Salter heard a story of an organization begun by enthusiasts, an organization which waxed and waned depending on the energy level of those involved in any given year, and whose records and artifacts were only now being given the loving care they deserved. The replica seemed to have disappeared in a slack year.

Salter found a bench in Connaught Square and sat down to compare the archives' photograph with the one recovered from Elton's house. Elton's was sharper, but it compared in every other respect with the replica. He studied the two pictures for several minutes wishing he knew more about photography, and went over the possibilities. He considered returning to the archives to find out if Elton had ever made a copy of the photograph, but decided that the answer would not mean much. If yes, then Elton might have taken a copy for comparison purposes; if no, it proved only that Elton's semi-official status might have allowed him to make a copy without the archivist's knowledge. Salter considered calling on Croll to let him know that they had both had the same idea, but first he returned to the Historical Society and borrowed a magnifying glass through which he examined the pictures again. It occurred to him as he was doing so that this was the first time he had ever used that classic instrument of detection, and he hoped Croll would not walk in while he was there and treat himself to a big laugh.

When he was satisfied, he drove back to Marlow. Outside Elton's cottage an RCMP station-wagon was parked and Salter stopped beside it. The constable inside was new to him, but he knew Salter by name and let him in. 'I was just making the place secure,' the Mountie said. 'The staff sergeant said we've finished in here but it's still our responsibility until the case is over.'

Nothing had been moved and Salter took one more slow look around the house before he got out of the Mountie's way and allowed him to lock the front door. 'Tell Fehely I was looking for him, will you?' he said, and went home for lunch, brooding over what he had found. He wanted to take one more step, one that would involve a professional photographer, but he would find what he wanted only in

Charlottetown. He was in no hurry to make a fool of himself.

That afternoon he drove Annie to Charlottetown to visit her sons, and began the search for a photographer. He found one, then checked himself. The story of the seal was known to everyone, and he was not yet ready for the photographer's questions, so he tucked the pictures away and called on Croll instead.

CHAPTER 13

He found the staff sergeant in his office.

'I think it may have been someone in cahoots with Brady. Some kind of double-cross,' Croll said.

'Maybe. Your story of the seal being worth twenty thousand dollars might have set a couple of thieves at each other.'

'One of them was Brady, all right. The report on the jewellery is in, and we've even got a print of Brady's on one of the spoons.' Croll turned a piece of paper round so that Salter could read it.

'What's this?' Salter asked, looking at a separate piece of paper clipped to the first.

'Lab report on the sack. There was no human blood on it, just chicken blood. No that it matters.'

Salter said, 'When was that chicken house used last? For killing chickens?'

'Why? Ten years. Maybe fifteen. The old guy who owned the place and sold it to the professor hadn't worked it for that long. Didn't you notice? The field out behind the barn was nearly back to bush again.'

'How long does the smell of chicken stay around? That bag wasn't ten years old. It smelled like it had been used last week, and left in the sun.'

'What are you telling me?'

'I'm telling you you ought to be looking for a chicken farmer.' He paused. Angus's fantasy rolled through his brain lighting up the connections between the points like an illuminated tourists' map of a subway system. 'The lava man,' he added, and explained.

Croll shouted for a constable and the three of them piled into a cruiser and headed for Tracadie and Gush's farm. But they were too late again. Tom Gush had been gone for two days.

They caught up with him next day in a motel in Maine. It had not been difficult because so many people remembered the strangely-coloured Canadian buying gas, or food, and crossing the border. And when the Maine state troopers burst into his room, the one with the truck parked outside with the PEI plates on it, they found Gush sitting on his bed where he had been all day, holding a shotgun. He surrendered without any fuss, with relief, it seemed, and Croll sent a couple of men to bring him back.

He called Salter to join him. 'We're holding him at Sleepy Hollow,' Croll said. 'Come down to the office and we'll go over there now.'

'How did he get past your man on the ferry?' Salter asked as they drove to the jail.

'We were looking for suspicious characters,' Croll said. 'Gush goes over all the time. He peddles lobsters to a highway stand in New Brunswick.'

The director of the jail lent them a room and sent for Gush, who arrived, casually escorted, a few minutes later. He nodded to Salter. 'I thought youse was on holiday,' he said.

'Sit down, Tom,' Croll said. 'Tell us your story.' He switched on a tape-machine.

Gush began immediately. 'I wish to confess to killin Jim Brady,' he said. 'Also Mr Elton.'

'Elton first,' Croll's voice said. 'Repeat this first, though.'

Gush read a statement that he knew he didn't have to answer any questions and that he had a right to have a lawyer present, but he waived these rights. 'Let's get on with it,' he said. 'I didn't mean to kill Mr Elton. I was in a tizzy with him coming in the door at me and me red-handed, so I hit him to get him out of the way so I could get out of there. I didn't mean to kill him, just get him out of the way.'

'But you did strike him?'

'I did strike him, yes.'

'What with?'

'The bar as I used to jimmy open the door. I still had it in me hand because I hadn't had time to give a proper look round.'

'Where is it?'

'In me truck. It's clean, though. It won't help you. I washed it off after. But that don't matter now, do it?'

'What were you doing in the house?'

'I was robbing it, wasn't I? Or trying to.'

'Had you ever done this before?' Croll was doing no more than pressing the button lightly to keep the flow coming.

'Yes. I have robbed a number of houses.'

'Which ones?'

There followed a long list of the houses Gush could remember having robbed. Eventually he said, 'That's it, I think.'

'What about the Watsons' place, and the Duggans'?'

'Oh yes. Them too.'

Here Croll looked at Salter. 'That's a complete list.' He turned back to Gush.

'Was anyone else involved with you in the robberies?'

'Yes. Jim Brady.'

Salter thought of the endless pressure that was usually necessary to get a suspect to talk like this. Listening to Gush was like overhearing someone dictate his memoirs.

'What part did Brady play? Did he go with you on some of the robberies?'

'No. He got rid of the stuff, and he told me when some of the places was empty.'

'He never actually participated in the robberies?'

'Eh? Oh no. He was too goddamn smart for that, wasn't he? No, I did all the dirty work. He took half the money.'

'Why? What did you need him for?'

'I had to, didn't I? The sonofabitch was blackmailing me.'

'How?'

'He caught me one night. He saw me coming out of the Owens' place. The next day he come up to me house and told me. He wanted to go into partnership. I had to go along.'

'What was he doing near the Owens' place?'

'What the bastard was always doing—coming or going from some woman.' Here Gush's voice took on a rough edge. 'That's all he ever did, did you know that?'

'Did he talk to you about it?'

'Sure he did. All the damn time. He was always boasting about it. And worse.'

'Worse?'

'Yes, worse. He used to get at me about it. He knew I never had no woman. Look at me. I had a wife for a little bit but she run away. I'm lucky if I can find a woman to take me money in Charlottetown. He used to tease me about it. Dirty rotten bastard. I'm not sorry I killed *him*, at any rate. Mr Elton, I am.'

'So you killed him because he was teasing you?'

'No. He stopped that when he saw I'd had enough. He knew when he'd gone too far.'

'But you did kill him.'

'Yes, I told you. I don't think I meant to, though. I don't know what I meant to do, but we pushed and pulled with that shotgun until it went off.'

'He was shot in the back of the head.'

'Was he? I don't know. We was rolling about and he tried

to get it off me, but he's a bit of a rabbit and I give him a push and the gun went off. That's how I remember it.'

'What happened first? Why were you on the farm?'

'It's where I used to put the stuff. In the chicken house. Then he would come along and take it away and sell it. He was very careful about not being seen with me in case I got caught eventually.'

'So what happened that night?'

'It was after I killed Mr Elton and the papers had the story about that seal that was worth twenty thousand. He'd been up to the farm and not found it, and he told me he knew I had it and he wanted it. With Mr Elton dead he had a proper blackmail going, didn't he? So he said he wanted me to hand it over, and he wouldn't believe me that I didn't have it. So I told him I'd hidden it in the farmhouse and I would meet him and show him. That's how it was. He'd been up first, though, and turned the place upside down looking for it.'

'You went to meet him with the gun?'

'Yes. I din't have killing him in mind, I don't think, but I'd reached my limit. I was thinking of turning meself in just to put a finish to it, the blackmail, the wondering if they'd catch me. You, I mean. I was going to tell Brady that, so I took the gun in case he turned nasty on me.'

'You had decided to confess to Elton's death?'

'I was thinking of it. It was only manslaughter, wasn't it, and I thought it might be better to take me punishment than have Brady round me neck for the rest of me life. I knew he wouldn't like it because he was involved in the robberies and that. So I took the gun, just in case. When he saw me with the gun he ran into the barn before I could tell him. I went after him and he grabbed me as I come in the door. That's when it happened.'

'So you killed him. What then?'

'I didn't mean to kill him. I don't think I honestly did. I

just wanted to show him I was serious. I think that's what
it was.'

'Then what?'

'Then I ran into the bush and hid for a little bit, but when
no one come I decided to get rid of him. I used his truck. I
drove down to Miminegash and found a boat, and I rowed
out for about an eighth of a mile, out to where the current
is, and I dropped him over.'

'Did you tie a weight on him?'

'Yes. I tied the anchor round his waist. I thought that
would keep him down for as long as necessary, but I had to
shorten the rope to keep him close to the bottom and I must
have done a poor job of tying it up again. It come loose,
didn't it?'

'You stayed around for a while after Brady's body was
recovered. Why did you decide to run in the end?'

'It was all the questioning. At first I thought I was all
right but your men was coming round every day, day after
day, questioning me, questioning everybody. I didn't know
but what I'd been seen, especially coming back from
Charlottetown, and I thought you'd find someone who'd
seen me in the end.'

'Charlottetown?'

'Yes. See, I drove Brady's truck into Charlottetown so
that you fellas wouldn't look for him around St Louis. I
thought I'd put you off the track, like. But then I had to get
back to get my truck, so I waited till morning and got a ride
with a driver that was headed up to Tignish. You never
questioned the driver because he was from away. But the
more I thought about it, the more I got frightened that
someone would have seen me or my truck, or the driver
would come back to the Island and hear about the case and
remember me. And all the time you fellas was questioning
and questioning and I knew they'd get to me in the end.'

Croll smiled at Salter.

'So where were you planning to run to?' he asked.

'I don't know.' Gush's voice was low and miserable. 'Anywhere away from here.'

'When they caught you, you were holding the gun. Why?'

'Was I? I expect I was thinking of doing meself in. I often thought of that.'

There was a pause, then Croll resumed briskly, 'All right. Now where's the seal?'

Gush's voice screamed out in an explosion of rage. 'I don't know where the goddamn, sonofabitching seal is. I never saw no seal, not in Mr Elton's house or anywhere else. I don't think the goddamn seal exists. I think you fellas invented it just to make people try to remember things about that night. That's what I think.'

'Invented it? For what?'

'Yes. Bloody invented it. Youse fellas. Or something's going on I don't know anything about. I told you I never had much chance to look around before Mr Elton came in, and I NEVER SAW NO FUCKING SEAL.'

As Gush's misery increased, the violence surfaced, and Salter had no difficulty imagining him as a man who responded to impediments by smashing them down.

'Okay.' Croll continued for a few minutes, getting the details of how Brady sold the stuff, then switched off and called the guard in. The two policemen watched as Tom Gush shuffled out of the room, saying nothing until his footsteps faded along the corridor.

Then Croll said, 'Poor bastard. You have to believe him, don't you? I do.'

'He smashed Elton's head in with an iron bar,' Salter reminded him.

'He panicked.'

'So do grizzlies if you startle them. That's why you stay away from them. He's a wild man, Brian.'

'He'd've been okay if he hadn't run into Brady.'

Now Salter saw Croll's view of the situation. Gush was an Islander sucked out of his depth by some 'sleazy bastard from away', Brady, the real criminal. Any Island chauvinist could see that. 'Now what?' he asked.

'I've got what I wanted. I feel sorry for the guy. And if, by any chance, we can manage a manslaughter on Elton and an accidental homicide for killing Brady, the sentence could be variable depending on whether the judge thinks he still has the seal and plans to sell it when he gets out. It might make quite a difference to his sentence. So I'd like to find the seal, not for your father-in-law's sake, but just so Tom Gush can tell his story and have it believed.'

'What do you plan to do?'

'First of all, I'll go over that farm with a Geiger counter, dig up every inch if I have to. The same with Tom's place, and the same with Elton's, just in case there's a cute hiding-place that you and I missed. At least if I don't find it I shall be able to tell the judge that I don't think the seal ever came to the Island. That'll help Tom a bit.'

'Is that how you think it will work out?'

'Yes, I do. Got any other ideas?'

'Just the picture. It's been bothering me.'

'How?'

'Go along with me for a while, will you?'

For the next couple of hours Salter led an amused Croll back over his tracks. First they went to Croll's office, where Salter produced the picture from the archives.

'I've already got one of those,' Croll said.

'I know.' Next Salter produced the copy found in Elton's house.

'I've got one of those, too,' Croll said. 'And I've had the boys here compare them. They aren't the same. You're wrong, Charlie. It was the second thing I thought of, when I found there was a picture in the archives. First I thought it was the same, then I thought it might have been doctored up. But the boys here say no. Surprised?'

'No. You got a flash camera around?'

It was Croll now who looked surprised. 'I could find one.'

'Borrow one for an hour.'

'Where are we going?'

'Elton's house, to start.' Salter refused further comment. At Elton's house they retrieved the original folder of pictures that included the picture of the seal, and this time they found the complete set of negatives, including that of the seal. 'That's what's been bothering me,' Salter said. 'The pictures of the seal were part of a roll taken on the Island. Look at these others; look at this one. Elton's fiancée, isn't it?'

'But Elton didn't take those pictures,' Croll said. He was puzzled and angry. 'Those pictures were sent by Callendar.'

'After Elton sent them to him.'

'Elton was in on a scam with Callendar?'

'Look where the pictures were developed.' Salter pointed to the name on the envelope, that of a printing house on Yonge Street in Toronto. 'Elton had them developed and gave them to Callendar to be sent to him.'

'Nah, you've got it wrong. Elton must have taken his camera to Toronto, took the pictures in Callendar's shop, got them developed and left the roll with Callendar. I was right. The seal never came to the Island. Callendar's still got it.

'Maybe.' Salter stood up, the picture of the seal in his hand.

'Right, Salter? The seal exists but it never came here. Right?'

Salter walked upstairs to the bedroom, followed by Croll. On the wall above the bureau he found again what he was looking for. 'Hang on,' he said to the importuning Croll. 'I'll be with you in a minute.' He went downstairs to retrieve the camera from the car, and returned to take some pictures of the bedroom wall. 'Okay,' he said. 'Now let's go back to your photographer.'

'You're out of your skull,' Croll said, when Salter explained what he was thinking.

Once more it took the photographer a few minutes only to confirm what Salter had guessed, that the picture he had taken of the bedroom wall was identical to the background of the original picture, complete with a nail-hole and two small specks of dirt.

Back in his office Croll said, 'Then the goddamn thing *is* here, or was, if Elton took the picture. So where the hell is it?'

'My guess would be that it never left the Island. You remember when you asked Callendar how big it was, how much it weighed, how it was wrapped, you remember it took him some time to respond. All the performance he went through trying to remember if it was wrapped in canvas or what. I don't think Callendar ever saw the seal in his life.'

'So tell me what you *do* think.'

'I think Elton got hold of the seal on the Island, identified it, saw an opportunity for himself and fixed up the rest with Callendar. Never mind the legal position of anyone else finding it. In Elton's position he would have *had* to hand it over.'

'Let's go get Callendar. Find the fucking seal.'

'Hold on. He may not know where it is.'

'I'm going to tweak his nose, though, just to be sure.'

'What's Callendar done that's illegal? He was offered an opportunity to negotiate a sale for an anonymous client. So he did. He was approached by mail, and that's how he approached the government. Then Elton came in—brought in by my father-in-law, by the way—to negotiate his own scam. But Elton probably set up the idea of a Marblehead client, and Callendar just did what he said he did.'

'Come off it, for Christ's sake. You think Callendar didn't know what was going on? Don't give me that.'

'Sure he knew. All I'm saying is that Callendar might have

been smart enough to stay at arm's length. His story still holds together.'

'But he came down when Elton was killed and he sure as hell acted like someone who believed the killer had the seal which Elton had brought back.'

'But his story is still good. An anonymous client delivered the seal to him, and he delivered it to Elton. Everything he did after that is consistent with his story, including asking to be compensated. He couldn't exactly sit back and say, "Oh well. Too bad". But if you can prove the seal never left the Island you've got him on some kind of fraud. At any rate, there's enough doubt now so that I can tell Montagu not to pay up, which is all I care about.'

Croll passed his finger under his bottom lip. 'I may not be able to prove it, so I may have to try a little bluff.' After a few more minutes of reflection and doubt, he picked up the phone and called Callendar, telling him they had now located the seal and suggested that Callendar return to the Island to establish ownership. It worked, and Callendar promised himself on the first plane the next day.

Croll put down the phone. 'Three o'clock tomorrow, Charlie. Come and watch.'

CHAPTER 14

Piece by piece Croll laid before Callendar the evidence they had gathered. Callendar stuck to his story for a long time, maintaining that he had received the seal from Marblehead, delivered it to Elton on the Saturday, and that any shenanigans were entirely Elton's doing.

'You say that the seal was wrapped in canvas,' Croll said. 'What colour?'

'Canvas-coloured of course. Isn't all canvas the same colour?'

'Some is darker than others. Was this dark or light?'

'About medium.'

'What held the canvas together? Was it sewn on?'

'Yes. I told you that.'

Croll nodded. Then he said, 'Clive Elton was met at the airport by his fiancée. He was carrying a little overnight bag which she put in the back of her car. They went to his house so that he could change, but he didn't take the bag out of the car. He didn't take the bag home with him when he left her that night. It was still in her car when Elton was killed. We have it now. There was no seal in the bag. He never brought it back. You want to tell us again exactly how it was wrapped, and how big it was, and how much it weighed?'

'I want a lawyer,' Callendar said, his sparkle dimmed.

'Sure you do. But you want to tell us your story anyway?'

Callendar looked at Salter, who shrugged. 'It might help,' he said, admiring Croll's invention and reminding himself that he had seen the bag in Elton's closet.

'All right.' He told the whole story then, of how Elton had approached him with the seal, of how Elton had manu- factured a Marblehead dealer, at Callendar's suggestion, enabling Callendar to stay in a more or less legal position. And of how they had agreed that Elton would deliver the seal to Callendar and then publicly return with it the same day, going straight to Montagu's office. 'So,' ended a largely extinguished Callendar, 'when I heard that Clive was dead, I realized that if you found the killer *and* the seal, I would be in an odd position. It seemed wise, therefore, to tell the story as I did. You must admit, we were very unlucky.'

'Yes, you were. Why did you come down right away?'

'To identify it, of course, if it turned up. And to claim it.'

'That wasn't necessary. Your position was that you would get your commission if we found the thing.'

'I didn't think too clearly. Things were happening too quickly.'

'No.' Croll shook his head. 'There's someone else involved, isn't there? Some potato-farmer who got a hundred bucks from Elton and might come forward when he heard what it was worth. You hung around, got your picture in the paper, so he would come to you, didn't you?'

'I don't know what arrangements Elton made, but I thought that if whoever he got the seal from got a little more money he might stay quiet, yes.'

'You were hoping to be blackmailed.'

'Not for a sizeable amount.'

'Less than your commission.'

'Of course.'

'Did you also have another idea? That if someone else found the seal, he might come to you instead of the government, and get a little bit more than the reward. Then you could sell it again in ten years' time?'

'Good God, no. I wanted no part of the thing any more. I just wanted to keep the original transaction from getting out.'

'Okay. Forget about that. You and Elton were to get ten thousand each, right? Less whatever he paid for the seal.'

'Yes. What's the difference? The Island would have its seal and the price was fair. Less, anyway, than if someone from Marblehead had found it, because Clive wouldn't go for a really big price.'

'Unlike you.'

'Am I under arrest now?'

'Of course you are, or you will be. Get your lawyer and we'll do the same, find out what we can charge you with. In the meantime it might help if you tell us whatever else you know. Cooperate fully.'

'What else is there?'

'The government would still like the seal. Where did Elton get it?'

With this question, Callendar visibly relaxed. 'That I

don't know. He said someone had found it and brought it to him.'

'Who?'

'I don't know. He wouldn't tell me.'

'Think hard. Did he give you any clues? It's no worse for you if we find him, is it? If you are telling the truth it would confirm that Elton is the major actor. You just got caught out in a little lie, right? Just being foolish. A dumb accomplice.'

Callendar sparked up slightly. 'Yes, I was, wasn't I? A dumb accomplice.' He let the phrase roll through his teeth. 'He did mention something about it being fished up at one point, but I don't know whether he was speaking literally or not.'

Salter looked up. 'That why you were hanging around the harbours?'

'Yes. I couldn't think of anywhere else to hang about.'

'But no one came forward?'

'No.'

Croll said, 'All right, Mr Callendar. We'll keep you here until we arrange a bail hearing. I assume that's what you want?'

'I want a *lawyer*,' Callendar said, looking solemnly first at Croll, then at Salter.

Croll nodded and called for a constable to take Callendar to a telephone. When he was gone, Croll said wearily, 'All I have to do is question every fisherman on the Island again. Thanks, Charlie. Still, my case is wrapped up.'

But after a night's sleep Salter had an idea worth two of that, and he wanted to find the seal more than Croll did, so the next day he felt free, without telling Croll, to go down to the harbour just before two o'clock where Joe 'n' Eddie were preparing their boat for the afternoon's outing. Salter took Joe aside and began by asking him if he would mind delivering a small cod to the house the next day.

'We don't deliver, Mr Salter. You know that. We're not

fishmongers, not even for Mr Montagu's family. You want fish you can come down and buy it when we bring it in.'

'You delivered to Mr Elton though, didn't you?'

'How do you mean?'

Salter stopped beating about the bush. 'The morning I was at Elton's house you came by on your way to work. You told me and the Mountie you were just calling to see if Mr Elton wanted some fish delivered. You don't deliver fish, and you sure as hell don't call in for orders on your way to work. You were calling to see when he wanted the seal delivered, weren't you? Where is it now? On your boat?' Salter nodded to where Eddie was washing down the deck, watching them.

'Why don't you search it? Or get that Mountie fella who's been hanging around the dock. He'll do it.'

'Not if you don't mind. Where is it?'

Joe looked around the harbour and motioned Salter over to the wall. The two men sat down. 'You've got a nerve, haven't you?' Joe said. 'Accusing me, just because I happened to make an exception of Mr Elton. I wanted to do him a favour. He was a nice man.'

'Was he? Did you know he was going to get ten thousand for that seal?'

'It wouldn't surprise me. And if that surprises *you,* then let me remind you that Mr Elton was a decent man. Things are done different on the Island than where you come from, mebbe.'

So Elton had been fair with Joe 'n' Eddie, which was another reason why Callendar had been wasting his time.

Joe watched Salter take in the information he had just packaged and delivered. 'So where's the seal?' Salter repeated.

'Hang on a minute. I'll just see if Eddie needs a hand.' Joe got up and went over to his brother, and the two men chatted for a few minutes. Eddie shook his head at first, then shrugged and went back to washing the deck. Joe returned to sit beside Salter. 'No, he's all right,' he said. 'Now what was it you was asking me?'

'Where's the seal?'

'I don't know what the hell you're talking about, but if it's about that thing that's been in the papers, here's how we've been speculatin', Eddie and me. Supposing someone was dragging for ground-fish and he brought up something interesting, like. It happens now and again. And suppose he was told it was worth a few dollars and to keep quiet about it, see. He might put it away, safe, like, and after a bit it turns out that he might be able to get as much as five thousand dollars for the thing—I'm just speculating. Now that's a lot of money, isn't it? But then the man who's been arranging things for him gets killed one night, and it looks as though this thing had something to do with it.'

'That was an accident. It didn't have anything to do with the seal.'

'Not at the time. But it did after, didn't it, because when the Mounties started looking for the man who killed Mr Elton, they was looking for the man who had the seal? Am I right?'

'You could be.'

'So I could. So whoever the police find with the seal is the man who killed Mr Elton, the way they would see it. Do you take my point?' Joe waited for Salter to nod before he continued. 'He'd have a bloody funny story to tell the police, from their point of view, of how this fella who was killed never did have the object, except p'raps for a couple of hours, because it was with the first fella all the time. Do you follow me?'

Salter nodded solemnly.

'And then a little later another fella is killed, and there's talk that he might have had something to do with this object, too. Well, I'll tell you, Mr Salter, one way and another there's a bit too much blood on this object for the taste of the average fella around here, and what with the suspicion and all, what do you think he would do?'

'Get rid of it?'

'That's what we think, too. Me and Eddie.'

'Where?'

Joe's gaze wandered out to sea.

'Put it back where he found it?' Salter asked.

'That's what we was wondering. We think that object is about two miles out in the Gulf, and there it will stay.'

'Was it in the truck when you called on Monday morning? Were you delivering it so that Mr Elton could take it to Toronto later?'

'I don't know what you're talking about. I'm just telling you what we was speculating about. That dealer fella was talking to every fishing-boat owner on this side of the Island, and there was the Mountie, follering him around, so we put two and two together. But apart from that I don't know nothing. I made an exception with Mr Elton in the way of delivering a bit of fish to him occasionally, because he was a very decent fella. Eddie would tell you that.'

'What about his cleaning lady? Would she be able to confirm it? That you delivered fish to him?'

'Oh, I doubt it. We asked Mr Elton to keep it strictly between us so you wouldn't all be asking for the same thing.'

'And all this is just you speculating, is it?'

'That's right. I wouldn't want the Mounties to put any faith in it, though. Let 'em keep looking.' Joe stood up, and carefully removed his hat, revealing a head of thick, lustrous, wavy brown hair. He wiped the sweatband carefully with a handkerchief, replaced his cap and walked off to join Eddie.

'You think he's telling the truth? What if I don't do anything and the thing turns up next year in Marblehead?' Croll asked.

'Not a chance. Not unless someone goes out with a diving bell.'

'Your father-in-law agree?'

'Yeah. He's sad about it, but he agrees.'

'In that case . . .'

'I know—fuck it.'

There were only five days of the holiday left. Eleanor Vail was still recovering from the shock of Brady's death, and preferred to be left alone. Angus had disappeared. 'He's chasing a girl at the Yacht Club,' Annie explained. Fehely's girlfriend insisted that now he was getting some time off again he spend it with her, so Salter was left alone with Annie. 'What would you like to do?' he asked her.

'She said, 'You know another thing you have never suggested?'

'Salter racked his brains. 'What?'

'Teaching me to fish. Every year we've come here you've wandered around looking for someone to play golf with, but you never offered to teach me. Now you are going to learn fly-fishing.'

'You never asked me to take you out golfing, either.'

'That's because I thought it was a great big deal. Would ruin your holiday. Until you offered to teach Eleanor.'

'Jesus Christ. Of course I will. You learn to play golf *and* fish and this place would be terrific.'

It could be, too, thought Salter, in the afterglow of the best time he had ever had on the Island. With harness-racing, fly-fishing, and a wife who played golf, a man could have a fine time, even without a couple of murders.

Two days later, when he was beginning to get the hang of fly-fishing, Salter and Croll had one last conversation about the seal.

'I was talking to a friend of mine in the Fisheries Department,' Croll said. 'Just in general terms, about this and that. This friend of mine told me something I thought you might like to hear. He said that Joe 'n' Eddie never drag for

ground-fish. They don't have the right equipment, because
they don't fish that way off the North Shore. And another
thing. If that seal went into the sea, it would have been off
the South Shore, near Charlottetown where the raiders came
in.'

'What do you make of that?'

'Not much. I still think that the seal is out in the Gulf
somewhere, where Joe 'n' Eddie dumped it, but I don't
think that's where they found it.'

'So what are you going to do about it?'

'Nothing. But for our own curiosity, I hope that Joe or
Eddie one day, on his deathbed, maybe will whisper the
secret of where the thing was found.'

'There's lots of time. You're retiring here, aren't you?
Maybe Joe will take you into his confidence in another
twenty years. He'll forget you're from away. Now. Stand
back while I show you a real cast.'